His hand went through the form on the bed, sinking into a dampness that made him scream.

His hand must have reached for the light without his thinking about it, because the room was suddenly flooded from the bedside table lamp, and Sylvia, looking startled and sleepy but otherwise okay and unharmed, sat upright in the bed.

"Oh my God, Tim! What's wrong?"

"I...I—" His wild gaze scanned the room. What had just happened to him? What was going on? There was no blood there—not on the bed, nor the floor, nor even in what he could see of the hallway. He was baffled. Had it really been another vision, so close on the heels of the last two? If so, these were so different than any he'd had before. These were...intrusive, disrupting his reality. For the first time in decades, he felt genuinely scared of them.

"I thought—I thought I saw blood and—and my hand went through you and...*Christ.*"

She searched his face. Seeming to find real fear there, she pulled him gently into a hug. He buried his face gratefully in her hair, inhaling the scent of her, holding on tightly.

"What happened tonight?" she asked softly in his ear.

THE
SHAPES
OF
NIGHT

MARY SANGIOVANNI

My Patreon supporters—thank you.

ACKNOWLEDGMENTS

Mary would like to thank Michael and Suzanne SanGiovanni, Michele and Mike Serra, Christina SanGiovanni, Ada SanGiovanni, Seedling and Seedlet, and Brian Keene.

She would also like to thank Paul Goblirsch and the good folks at Thunderstorm, as well as all the Patreon patrons who motivated her and supported her through the writing of this book.

ONE

The night that it started, Tim Jenkins walked into the screaming mouth of sin to save a tall, skinny fang of a boy from a nebulous but probable death.

The mouth belonged to a club called 138, a place that belched out a noxious breath of pot and cigarette smoke, spilled beers, and damp sweat. It growled old-school punk music from the back of its throat and vomited the occasional stumbling drunk. There was no bouncer at the front door. Those who entered knew what they were going into. Those who wandered in without a clue were on their own.

Club 138 was one of the only places like that in the area.

When the kids wanted booze, they went a couple of towns away to Wexton. When they wanted drugs, they went to the City (New York City, that was, but the kids in northern New Jersey just called it "the City"). When they wanted trouble, they went to Club 138.

Charlie Bentner's friends were almost always looking for some kind of trouble. But it was late June and school was out (for the summer, forever, in Charlie's case), and technically, Charlie and his friends weren't Tim's problem anymore. Tim had finished up the last of his paperwork and handled a few late grades to sway an Incomplete to a Pass or Fail. He'd attended the end-of-the-year meetings. He'd cleaned out his classroom of the remnants of old students. He was done with school, too, at least for a couple of months. He'd been looking forward to watching sitcoms over a beer while Sylvia curled up on the couch alongside him, and maybe later, some goodnight sex with the windows open and mild night breezes blowing across his back and cooling their sweat.

The headache came halfway through *Everybody Loves Raymond*, a dull thudding that blurred his vision so that the flashing pictures behind his eyes could take precedence. A low rushing like ocean breakers filled his ears, blocking out all sound. He'd seen Charlie Bentner folded in half against some kind of brick wall. A sticky wooden bar whose gouged surface was littered with empty bottles. A tattoo of a Betty Page-ish demoness. Blood dripping onto pale pavement. Tattoo of a dragon skeleton about to devour something from the palm of a skeletal claw. Pale-faced children-things drenched crimson, peeling patches of inked skin off a raw-meat form curled in on itself on the ground and shaking as if seized by intense cold. More blood, splattered black against a green dumpster. A door cracked open enough to see a universe behind it. More blood.

The flashes happened very infrequently, but when they did, they came as a rapid firing of images that made little sense on their own. Usually, they told him of a sick family member's impending death or an upcoming traffic disaster that would result in multiple accidents. They were always vivid enough to justify the headache. They had never been as gruesome—or as strange—as the one about Charlie Bentner.

Then the flashes stopped and the canned laughter of the sitcom seeped into his ears again, and he mashed a fist into his tearing eyes. To his right, Syl hovered, worried, one hand on his shoulder and the other rubbing his back. She knew about the snapshots—that's what she called his mental snippets of vision, and he was inclined to agree that "snapshots" were exactly what they were. Blurred faces, disturbing close-ups, random objects, all out of focus, they were snapshots taken by some really bad photographer, and he often wondered whether or not they'd be any clearer if he had a better handle on the mental camera equipment.

He didn't—they simply came and went as they had since he was twelve. He couldn't control them or start or stop them from happening, and Sylvia knew that, too. She didn't have to ask what was wrong. He told her anyway.

"It's one of my kids. Charlie Bentner. I don't know—"

"Then go find out," she replied softly. "Wake me when you get back."

So he'd taken a stab at which place might boast a sticky, scored bar and also the kind of crowd that Charlie might hang with. He'd driven to Club 138 and sure enough, there was the twins' truck, and behind it, Jeremy's car. Charlie's friends were there, and so Charlie probably was, too.

It had been Tim's experience teaching high school for the last eight years that there were different types of fringe teens. "Fringe" sounded better, he supposed, than "troubled" or "bad." They weren't all bad, really. Some of them had just been dealt a bitch of a hand in life, not unlike Tim himself growing up, and he tried to remember that when one of them mouthed off to him in class or cut school or smoked in the hallway.

For some, behavior like that was more about posturing than actually causing any real trouble. These were the kids who found the idea of being bad boys and girls exciting and attractive. It gave them an identity, a sense of belonging. Tim got that. They were the most reasonable and most likely to grow out of the phase. Others were the perpetual bad-choice-makers, the ones, a colleague of his had put it rather brusquely, that were always stepping in shit because they refused to look where they were going. Cases in point were Charlie's friends, twin brothers John and Joseph McGovern, and a boy named Pete Degrassi. The twins were burnouts good for little more than ogling tits and laughing in that goofy Beavis-and-Butthead way they had, but they were harmless. Pete Degrassi, a kid in threadbare concert T-shirts and ripped jeans and the kind of long rock-star hair that was popular when Tim himself was a teen, wasn't much different. Those three boys were too stoned most of the time to be any real problem and were amiable enough to be herded through a five-year program of high school vocational-technical classes without too much incident.

The third type were the kids with home lives that made teachers like Tim cringe in sympathy and frustration and made other kinds of teachers give up on them as lost causes early on. These kids had low self-esteem and often, issues with making or keeping friends. They were often loners, often too smart or not smart enough to fit in. Some were content to fade into backgrounds until the grind of adult mediocrity eventually wore them down. Tim thought Charlie Bentner fit neatly into that category.

It was the fourth type which concerned Tim most of all, partly because the other types kept company with them and couldn't quite see them for what they were. Volatile anger and sometimes mental illness swallowed these kids whole. Sometimes they robbed liquor stores and shot clerks. Sometimes they shot up a school.

In Tim's profession, it had become important to know the difference between these types. It was sad, really—the kind of thing that made him want to retire more and more every year. It used to be that schools were a safe place to be, even when a kid's home life wasn't. A lot had changed in twenty-five years.

Afterimages of the snapshots accompanied him all the way to the club. He had considered calling the police all the way there, but what could he say? That he was having psychic visions that some children were going to hurt one of his students somehow, somewhere, for some nebulous reason? That had never worked too well for him before. In an area like Awayack, New Jersey, psychics were considered crackpots, and no one wanted crackpots teaching their precious children. No one gave crackpots tenure. So he'd learned to keep his mouth shut about the things he saw until he had something even remotely substantial to prove it.

As he pulled into the parking lot, Tim saw the McGovern brothers and Pete DeGrassi hanging by the front of the club beneath the ultraviolet Club 138 lights. They passed either a joint or a cigarette they'd rolled themselves between them; Tim wasn't sure which it was until he'd crossed the lot and gotten close enough to catch a whiff of the sweet and cloying smoke.

When they saw him, they dropped the joint and kicked it toward the wall behind their shoes. Coughing, John took a step forward while behind him, his brother swatted at the last wisps of smoke in the air before his face.

"Mr. Jenkins? Whatchoo doin' out here, man?" John's eyes, veined in red, blinked as if to bring him into focus.

"I'm looking for Charlie, guys. Is he here?"

Joe nodded, and nudged John, who nodded, too. "Inside."

The club was packed. He made his way through the wraith crowd of pale faces (*pale child-things*) and black clothes and glinting silver pins and chains. One tall, heavyset boy bowed his head and glowered up at Tim from heavily lined eyes, the phalanx of his black and green spired hair positioned in case the boy decided to charge him like a rhino. His arms were crossed over his chest, and Tim noticed he had a tattoo of a dragon skeleton about to devour something from the palm of a skeletal claw.

Tim edged past him along a gouged wooden bar and headed toward the back of the club, away from the bar, and the crowd gathered in the center around a stage. There was no live band tonight, but the crowd slam-danced to the music that hailed down on them from the speakers overhead.

He found Charlie and his crew at one of the booths in the very back of the club and hesitated. He had absolutely no idea what to say. *Charlie, I saw you die tonight. How about we blow this joint and I'll walk you home to make sure the dead children don't fold you in half?*

Dead children...why had he guessed that they were dead?

Simple, his mind told him. *You didn't guess. You know they're dead. Or something like dead.*

Tim shook his head, took a deep breath, and headed back toward Charlie and his friends.

Sitting on a chair just outside the booth, another of that stoned-but-harmless breed, Mike Schuyler, sat with his head tilted back and his eyes closed. Charlie said something to him and he frowned, sitting up and throwing his friend a look of sheer disbelief. He'd seen their banter before, in the hallways at school. In fact, Tim kind of liked their sarcastic wit and identified with them during the awkward moments of jostling with each other and impressing the skinny goth-waif girls in their social circle.

But Jeremy Clinton, to Charlie's right, was a different story. He wore a sense of cool calculation almost like a filmy second skin. Tim got the sense that Jeremy's eyes, a frosty blue, took in and processed everything through a grossly skewed perception, but they betrayed no excitement, no love or anger in any way. That was neither due to a lack of intelligence nor understanding but rather, a lack of remorse or empathy. Everything about him—his punk-spiked blond hair, the plumage of the alpha male in their crew, the carefully chosen symbols of his tattoos (one of which, Tim saw, was a demonic version of Betty Page), his jewelry, the cryptic messages of his T-shirts, even the deep pockets of his baggy pants—all suggested something hidden beneath the surface just waiting for the chance to flare out in a blinding burst of violence. Tim had seen others like him before and was sure he'd see others like him again. And he knew enough to be cautious of every one of them.

Mike spotted him first, and nudged Charlie.

"Hey, guys!" Tim shouted to be heard over the music and nodded at each in turn as he approached. Mike offered "Wassup" before turning away from him. Jeremy watched him carefully, a small smile on his face that was difficult to interpret in the smoky haze hanging over the table. But his eyes were clearly angry. He resented the intrusion.

Charlie offered a good-natured grin at Tim and flicked the ashes of his cigarette into a nearby ashtray. "Jenks. I didn't know you hung out here." Charlie's dark-brown hair hung to his shoulders and often dipped into his face, shielding his bright, intelligent green eyes when he was on the defensive. Tonight it was tucked beneath a black baseball cap pulled backward. His black T-shirt—one of many—glittered under the UV lights, the red writing (*Can't Sleep or the Clowns Will Eat Me*) repeated in shrinking letters down the length of the front. But his rumpled appearance aside, he exuded a kind of warmth that generally made girls trust him and teachers wonder how he'd fallen in with "that crowd." His attitude was balanced by his wit—a quality that Tim found fewer and fewer students possessed, sadly, with each new class.

"Charlie, I need to talk to you. In private, if possible."

Charlie rolled his eyes. "Jenks, come on, cut me a break. School's out. It's summer. We ain't on your watch anymore." Charlie raised his mug of beer, glanced at Tim and then at

Jeremy, seemed to think better of drinking in front of an old teacher, and put the mug down.

"It's important, Charlie."

"What's it about?" Jeremy's eyes challenged him.

Tim glanced at him uncomfortably and shifted his weight to his other foot. "Charlie, please."

"We're busy, Jenks. Waiting for one of Charlie's angels," Jeremy said.

"Yeah, she's supposedly here with some mother—" Mike caught himself and finished, "some dude."

"She's not mine," Charlie said, looking away.

Tim could feel the impending defeat, and his voice dropped. "Look, I know you're busy and I'm probably the last person you want to see right now, but this is really serious. Do you think I would have come out here, to this...place...if it wasn't?"

How important was it? Had his snapshots ever been wrong? He didn't think so...but Charlie had a point. These kids weren't his problem anymore...not really.

He was trying to talk himself into bailing on Charlie, bailing on the whole thing, but he wouldn't. He knew that. He couldn't. Charlie may have had a tendency to be in the wrong place at the wrong time with the wrong people, but he was basically a good kid.

Tim had once seen Charlie defend a special-ed student from a basketball player (*Go, Tigers!*) named Dave. The larger boy was knocking books out of the smaller boy's hands and slinging names like "retard" and "idiot" into the after-bell echo of the empty hallway. Charlie (who'd been cutting class, Tim discovered) had strode right up to Dave, a good head taller, and had gotten up in his face. Tim anticipated having to break up a fight, but the jock had backed off. When Dave was gone, Charlie had picked up the books and handed them to the boy, who took them gratefully. And although he didn't understand why Dave had been picking on him, he recognized that Charlie had done a Good Thing for him, and he hugged Charlie, who blushed and playfully shooed him onto class.

Charlie had turned then and stopped short when he saw Tim, a guilty look on his face like he'd been caught setting fire to something. "Brother at home like that," he'd muttered as he shouldered past and down the hall. Tim hadn't replied then, but it had carved a groove in his mind. Despite the company he kept, Charlie was the redeemable kind of fringe teen, the kind on the cusp of success or failure. Kids like him had hope and smarts and talent and genuine kindness, a conscience, and that slim chance to overcome whatever situations at home or otherwise put them in their current frame of mind. All too often, though, Tim watched those kids bend under the crushing weight of criticisms, of snap judgments, of assumptions and of self-fulfilling prophecy. That was the one thing Tim hated about his job—the fact that he had to let some of them go, just raise the white flag and admit defeat.

But the snapshots were a different thing. Those he couldn't let go. Maybe he couldn't save every kid from a dead-end job or early pregnancy or keep them out of jail or off drugs, but he'd be damned to sleepless nights and an even guiltier conscience if he didn't at least try to put those images together in some semblance of the big picture.

"Charlie?"

At first, he wasn't sure if the boy heard him. Something on Tim's face must have come across to the boy, though, because he frowned and exchanged glances with Jeremy, who slid out of the booth to let Charlie out.

Charlie followed Tim through the crowd until he saw that the other patrons of the club saw Tim as a non-entity whose way they could blithely block with their metal tips and spikes and whatnot. Tim shrugged at the boy behind him, and Charlie took the lead, shouldering a way for them both through the jostling bodies to the front door. They emerged into a night that had chilled, or else felt cooler for the lack of pressed flesh all around them and made their way to the side of the building. The twins and Pete were gone, and Tim was glad for that. It was less explaining he had to do.

"So, what can I do for you, Mr. Jenkins?"

It was hard to read Charlie's tone, so Tim ignored it.

"Look, I know this is going to sound crazy, but I need you to listen to me, and even if you don't understand, I think you're going to have to trust me."

Charlie raised a single eyebrow as if he didn't trust where this conversation was going.

"I think you're in danger. You and maybe your friends. Tonight, uh, this place isn't safe."

"What, you mean...like, the cops are coming?"

"No, I can't...I don't know exactly what they are, but I've been dreaming about them all week and tonight while I was awake, I saw them...and I saw you...and there was blood, and—"

"Mr. Jenkins, you're not making a lot of sense."

Tim could see as much from Charlie's expression. He sighed and tried again. "I get these...pictures sometimes, in my head. Pictures of things that happened already sometimes, but more often, they're pictures of things that haven't happened yet, but will. In the beginning, I used to misunderstand them—see, they're symbols for things rather than the things themselves— but I've gotten pretty good at guessing what they mean over the years, and I'm not usually wrong.

"You can think this is all bullshit if you want to, and that's okay. But I was never going to be able to sleep easy tonight if I didn't at least warn you about what I saw. Because this time, Charlie, it was bad, and I don't think all that blood was symbolic. I don't know exactly what it means, other than that if you stick around here, you're going to get hurt. Maybe worse."

Charlie considered all this for a minute. It was a lot to take in, Tim knew. Finally, the boy said, "Craig."

"Who?"

"Craig..." he gestured vaguely, "...Angie's Craig. The Craig she's seeing now. He's looking for me, I guess. It's a long story, but Angie and I used to be a thing. Then we weren't, then we were, back and forth, then she met Craig. Then we hooked up again. So he's pissed. That's why the guys were with me tonight. We were gonna...you know...talk to him."

Tim knew, sure. Talking wasn't going to be so much a part of it.

"Anyway, maybe that's what you saw—a fight. A brawl. Something like that?"

Tim appreciated that Charlie had just accepted the idea of

his old teacher having visions of the future. That had been the part Tim had expected having to wrangle over. Maybe Charlie was preoccupied already, or maybe it was Tim's tone. Maybe it was just something Charlie believed in already—Tim had noticed that fringe kids tended to accept fringe reality more readily than other people. Whatever the reason, Charlie seemed at least partially on board.

"It's possible, but I don't think so. I think it's—"

Worse than that was what Tim was going to say, but he never got the chance, because just then, a girl came flying out the front door into the middle of the street, screaming and crying. Her face and the ample offering of cleavage she was showing were streaked with blood. She kept staring in wide-eyed disbelief at the crimson that coated her hands as well, and she kept screaming, like something had dug down into the deepest well of her and carved an opening into a pit of madness, and now all of it was welling up and out of her.

Others came stumbling out a few moments later, bleeding from gashes in their heads or ribs. Several were on their cell phones, ostensibly calling the police.

"Go," Tim told Charlie as he rushed toward the gathering crowd, but Charlie followed close behind.

"Excuse me," Tim said to a tall, gaunt guy with long black hair. The skin around the guy's left eye looked chewed and a hand, missing its pinkie and part of the ring finger, shook badly as he studied it. He looked up, dazed, at Tim's voice.

"What's going on in there?" Charlie broke in behind Tim. "What's happening?"

"The shapes," the tall guy muttered. "The shapes have come."

And he sank to the ground, bleeding and muttering.

"What?" Tim reached for his shoulder. "I'm sorry, what? Who's in there?"

He could pick up snippets of stunned conversation from the others in the assembled crowd. They spoke on cell phones or to each other or themselves.

"They're killing people..."

"I don't know, they look kinda little kids—"

"I'mmm hurt. We're all hurt."

"Someone's got to help the others, they—"

Tim exchanged glances with Charlie, then watched the door. Although it looked as if most of the club had emptied out into the street and sidewalk, Charlie's friends hadn't come out yet.

"They're still in there," a girl's voice whispered. "Still in there with the shapes."

Tim turned to see a young girl next to him. Her blond hair had gone strawberry-pink from the blood in it, and when she turned her face fully to him, he could see she was missing an eye. He fought the gorge in his throat and turned to Charlie.

"We have to get out of—"

But Charlie was already heading toward the door.

"Shit," Tim said to himself, and followed after.

TWO

"Charlie! Charlie, wait!"

Tim caught up with the frantic boy by the coat check and grabbed his arm. The boy paused, but impatiently, and his eyes searched the bar room beyond.

"You can't just charge in there! We don't know what we're up—"

"I've got to find her. All of them—I just left them. I have to find them." Charlie's anxiety made the features of his face small and tight. He pulled free of Tim's grasp and moved toward the bar. Tim followed him into a scene of carnage unlike anything he'd ever seen.

The absence of music and talking in the bar created an eerily uncharacteristic quiet. It was like the silence that followed being shushed, the sound of human interaction interrupted violently and suddenly. It wasn't a cemetery silence, where voices and movement had long departed and even the stones slept in peace. It was crime scene silence, uneasy, violated, and it bothered Tim immensely.

No one had shut off the slow-motion red-dark-green-dark-blue-dark strobe that washed like a slow tide over the dance floor. It was feeble light, though, and cast little more than a surreal fever-dream pall on the bodies that lay strewn like old toys all over the floor. Tim felt his gorge rise looking at them. There were probably about twenty of them, all young, all probably scared in those last moments far beyond what the tattoos, leather, and metal spikes they hid behind could protect them from. Tim thought of their parents, wondering if they knew where their children were, if they were waiting up for the sound of a car or keys jingling in the door to signal a safe return home. He wondered if they even knew their children were out in the first place.

He thought of the high school protocol for tragedies, the suicide watches, the meetings with students and student counselors. How many of them were students at the local high school? How many had younger siblings who were? As he surveyed the damage, he found himself looking at body parts, though, rather than bodies. A pierced nose on the floor. Something that might have been an ear ringed with metal. A Doc Martens boot with some shin sticking out of it. A ragged piece of flesh like a fallen flag, with a tattoo of a dragon skeleton about to devour something from the palm of a skeletal claw.

There was blood, like in the visions; it was splattered on faces, mostly, and dripped from ears, eyes, and noses. But what gripped and twisted Tim's stomach as he followed Charlie from corpse to corpse were the positions of the bodies. They were bent in all the wrong ways, limbs splayed in directions limbs were never meant to go. Elbows were bent in the opposite direction, as were knees. Heads were twisted completely around. Dislocated shoulders made some of the bodies look folded in on themselves. Feet pointed backwards.

In every face, the eyes were open wide. The grim rictus of horror distorted the swollen mouths.

Charlie made an odd, choked noise then, and Tim followed his gaze to the body of Craig Norman. Tim felt his heart sink. The dead boy's eyes had already begun to take on the hazy cataracts of desiccation. His mouth was open, and a number of his front teeth were missing. His arm was folded back at the shoulder and up behind his head, and something about the effect struck Tim as being horrifically ludicrous, like Craig was making some distorted comedic gesture over his own head. Tim's eyes followed the length of the torso to the twist at the stomach; the bottom half of the boy had been completely turned backward in a way that suggested a snapped spine. His toes, now facing the floor, propped up his wrong-way legs so that they bent forward a little. Craig Norman was a grotesque, broken thing somehow smaller and less bloody than he should have been.

Tim shook his head, half in disbelief. What could have done so much damage to so many people in so short a time?

The nagging voice that occasionally preceded or followed the visions he had answered. *You know what did that. The shapes...the dead children-things.*

He didn't know that, didn't even know what that meant, he argued silently with the voice. Seldom were his visions literal; whatever had done this likely had a reasonable, although tragic, explanation.

No. This is different. You know that.

"Charlie, man," Tim said, more to move away from his mental argument, "hey...you okay?"

Of course, he wasn't; it was a stupid question. How could he be? Less than an hour ago, he'd been sitting and sipping drinks, waiting for the arrival of the mangled thing at his feet. Charlie offered a weak thumbs up, though, and silently moved on to the next body.

Tim stole several glances at Charlie as he moved between the bodies, trying to make out where the boy's head was. The boy was searching the faces one by one, looking, Tim supposed, for familiar ones—for a particular face, the girl Angie he had mentioned, that one of the boys had referred to as one of his angels. Charlie's own face wore a stoic expression that betrayed little, but his eyes misted over occasionally, and Tim could see his hands shook every time he had to touch one of the bodies to turn it over and move hair out of its face. Tim suspected it was sheer force of will holding Charlie together. This was trauma beyond the pale—certainly nothing Tim was prepared for, let alone a teenaged boy. However, Charlie wasn't about to leave without satisfying the anxiety that drove him, and Tim wasn't leaving without Charlie. Frankly, Tim wasn't sure what else to do besides examine the faces, and it made him feel helpless. He didn't like it.

Already he could hear sirens in the distance, and even if Charlie did find someone he recognized, there wasn't anything either of them could do for him or her now. They were in a room full of badly mangled dead teenagers, and that was going to look bad no matter how a person sliced it.

"Charlie..." Tim began. He couldn't find the words, though. If it were his friends or, God forbid, his wife, there would have been no incentive strong enough to drag him away until he made sure, until he knew...and after all, wasn't that same sentiment what had brought him down to the club in the first place, that desire to make sure things were okay?

"She's not here," Charlie said, his voice as shaky as his hands. However, relief softened his face. "I don't see Mike, either, or Jeremy or the twins or Pete. I guess they got out, thank God. As long as—"

Charlie frowned, and then the color drained from his face. Tim followed his gaze to the stage and his heart froze in his chest.

One of the children from his vision—if, in fact, it could be called a child at all—was staring at them. It looked to be about nine, girlish in its features, with long, straight, white hair. Its chalky white skin was what had given Tim the impression in his vision of a dead child, though there was a poisonous life pumping through its black little veins—Tim was sure of that. In fact, from the outer corners of eyes entirely enveloped in obsidian and the corners of the mouth, the skin was marbled with little spider-webbing of black.

The creature reminded him of a tiny mime—or more accurately, of a horridly painted little marionette which had cut itself loose of its strings. Its disproportionately large head and eyes atop the stiff little body supporting it certainly suggested something very doll-like to Tim, as did its odd anachronistic clothes. It wore an old-fashioned church-lady hat of faded gray, a charcoal-hued jumper over a white blouse, ruffly socks and black dress shoes.

It tilted its head as if it found them curious. Then it placed its hands around its stomach, one above, palm down, and the other below, palm up. There was a slight tearing sound and the fabric of the jumper ripped open. The colorless plane of the child's stomach pleated and split apart, and a mouth lined with jagged teeth parted to produce a wail whose throat funneled out beyond time and space itself. The silence of a hundred held breaths was broken, and the awful sound that filled the void

Mary Sangiovanni

drowned his mind in pictures so horrible they brought him physical pain. He sank to his knees, covering his ears, but the sound was everywhere, inside and outside his head. He felt a hand roughly grip his shoulder and yank him to his feet, tugging him backward toward the door. He chanced one more look at the child and his gaze connected with the interior of that terrible second mouth. In it, he saw a blackening sky with many moons and alien stars, a sky from someplace beyond the limits of humanity, and for one terrible second, he thought he'd tumble forward and fall into that mouth and keep falling, falling endlessly through that other sky.

Then the cool air hit him and he was outside again, standing next to a pale and shaking boy, a boy he knew…what was his name? What had happened? Where was he?

Charlie. That was the boy. Reality—his reality—came rushing back all at once.

"Y-you okay, Mr. Jenkins?"

Tim nodded slowly, breathing hard. "Go home, Charlie."

"Huh?"

The cop cars were pulling up in front of the building, the ambulances right behind them, and the news crews not far behind that. Tim nodded in the direction of the approaching chaos. "Go home. Call your girl. Call your friends."

"But—but what about—?"

"I'll come find you tomorrow. Your house, noon. We'll talk it through then."

Charlie stood there for several seconds, glancing uncomfortably in the direction of the oncoming police, before nodding. "Okay. Okay."

He jogged off toward the parking lot through the crowd of reeling teens, all lost in their own personal piece of the tragedy, then stopped, turning back to Tim. "Uh, thanks, Jenks. I'm…I don't know what the hell's going on, but I'm guessing it would have been a lot worse if you didn't…you know…" He seemed at a loss for words.

Tim nodded, waving him on. "My pleasure, Charlie. Now get. See you tomorrow."

Gratefully, Charlie nodded. He tried a smile, but it was

trembling and uncertain, like the rest of him. Then he turned back and disappeared into the crowd.

When he saw Charlie's car pull away without incident, Tim made his way through the crowd toward his own car. Had he thought things through, he'd have parked a block down; uniformed officers were just starting to cordon off the parking lot and prevent people from leaving. Others were rounding people up to take their statements. Tim let himself be shepherded along with a small group of crying teens, summoning what he'd come to think of as teacher-patience despite inwardly wanting to bolt. He was tired and probably in shock, his brain not fully processing the series of events which had followed since he'd left the warmth, comfort, and normalcy of his couch. He supposed he could explain his being there at all as a favor to Charlie's parents; he'd been checking up on their son, and as the boy's teacher, he felt obligated to locate and make sure his student was okay. He didn't have to mention the visions at all.

And as for the girl-creature, if "girl" was even the right word for it...as far as his statement would go, he'd keep it short and simple, enough truth to clear him and send him on his way and no more. The teens could talk about the "shapes" all they wanted; the cops would chalk it up to trauma. Tim wanted to get home to his wife. Between the visions and what he'd seen tonight, he was sure this incident was only the beginning, and it wasn't just Charlie in danger anymore.

It took about two and a half hours of waiting outside in what had become a drizzly, gray-smeared night and another twenty minutes or so to give his statement and exchange contact information with the detective in case any follow-up interviews would be required, before Tim was cleared to go. They seemed to have grudgingly accepted his story about a welfare check on a student, and for that, Tim was grateful. It wasn't far from the truth, really; he had come to check on a student. He simply substituted his catalyst for an in-person meeting with Charlie's mom. He couldn't claim a phone call because phone records would no doubt be checked; however, given the local rumors that Charlie's mom was perpetually drunk and in a state of slurred speech and mild confusion, it would be Tim's word against her probable blackout. The only part of Tim's statement that might not hold up under scrutiny was the idea that Charlie's mom cared enough or was even aware enough to have noticed Charlie missing. If she didn't want to look like a poster woman for child neglect, though, she'd agree that she must have gone over to Tim's out of maternal concern for her boy, who she obviously had something of a damaged relationship with.

Would the story come back to bite him? He'd have to cross that bridge when he came to it. It seemed a saner explanation, certainly, than claiming a vision compelled him to action.

As he trudged back to his car, he was surprised by how fatigued he felt. His eyes had become heavy with exhaustion and his limbs felt weighted down. He wasn't just tired. He was ready to fall face first onto the next soft surface and sleep until noon. He texted his wife as he let himself into his car to let her know he was okay, and then he pulled out into the street.

The little blue digital dashboard clock read 4:17 a.m. He yawned. At the rate he was going, the sun would be up before he got home. Right then, the world was a frosty pre-dawn blue-black. The streets were deserted; even the night people had gone to bed and the morning people weren't up yet. The world belonged to no one.

That's not entirely true, a little voice in his head told him as he fought to keep his eyes open. It was taking supreme effort, and even when he did manage to do so, his thoughts fuzzified to the point of mind-babble. *The world belongs to the shapes. You know. You've seen. The little girl, Ms. Circle. Mr. Rhombus. Mr. Triangle. Ms. Hexagon. Mr. Rectangle. Ms. Trapezoid. The world is theirs now. They want it to be theirs.*

What the hell was that about? He tried to focus only on driving but found it almost as difficult as keeping his eyes open. The shapes. That's what the kids outside the club had called whatever attacked them in there, whatever mangled those bodies. The shapes. It made no sense, though. How had the patrons of Club 138 known what had attacked them? How had some made it out, while others hadn't? Had the arrival of that girl-creature, that shape, altered something in their minds?

Tim supposed it was possible that the events of the night were melding into each other the way dreams did, that his synapses were crossing their wires or something. In fact, maybe his brain had gotten a head start on processing everything through sleep before his body could catch up. He had to admit to feeling an increasing sense of dream-like surreality. Was that because of the girl-creature, too? Had she drugged him somehow? For all his thoughts' flights of strangeness, he found it hard to think too hard or feel too much about any one thing.

A dull, pounding ache began to throb above his left eye. He shook his head, rolling down the window in hopes the cooling air might rouse him a little.

It was then that a figure loomed up out of the sidewalk shadows, close to the street. Tim felt sure in that second that whoever it was meant to jump out in front of the car, and he swerved a little before realizing it was a mailbox. His heart pounded, and he swore under his breath.

Something was wrong. His head felt more than heavy with sleep; his vision was fuzzy and he was having trouble putting together even simple thoughts now. This wasn't like being tired; this was like being stoned. He wondered again if the girl-thing had done something to him, but he couldn't hold on to the thought for very long.

The broken yellow lines in the street peeled off the pavement and smacked against his windshield like debris caught in the wind. He flinched. As each one slid off, it made a little squeaking noise and left a faint smear of yellow.

Tim pulled over. The ache in his head had spread pretty quickly to the base of his skull and under his eyes and it was making him feel nauseous. What was happening to him? He closed his eyes and opened them. His brain felt like clay being stretched and folded, squashed and reshaped, and each motion sent pulses of pain through his body. He considered calling his wife but didn't want to worry her. Besides, he couldn't quite remember where he put the phone, or whether or not her number was even in it.

In the midst of the mental chaos, he felt a vision coming on.

In it, he was driving late at night. The roads were dark; all the street lamps were turned off, as were the house and store lights of the unfamiliar town he was driving through. The girl-thing from the club was sitting primly in the passenger seat, her eyes fixed on the road. When she turned to him, she had Charlie's face although he had no eyes. His mouth was caught in a frozen, silent scream and the dark sockets, which had gathered up so much of the night around them, bled a thick dark ichor down the cheeks. In the vision, Tim swerved. Then the images came to him in rapid, broken succession:

A small, abandoned house engulfed in blinding light.

A book whose bloody type inched and squirmed off the page.

A pale, chalky face of a young child...he knew the boy, but it was hard to make out the details...

A wild-haired hippy-man in a room crowded with maps and papers, peeling off wide strips of his own flesh as if it were paper; in fact, the undersides had words printed on them, though Tim couldn't read what they said...

A flash of light jolted him finally into clear-headed wakefulness. He glanced around. He was still in the driver's seat of his car, but his car was parked in the driveway. How had he gotten home? He couldn't remember. After a moment, he realized he was shaking all over and sweating profusely, but he felt solid again, righted somehow. He got out of the car, locking it behind him, and stumbled to the house. As he was about to fit the key in the door, he noticed the blood seeping out from under the door.

THREE

The key in the lock sounded deafening in Tim's ears as he let himself into the house. His attention was focused on the blood, which, as he opened the door, he saw had pooled just over the threshold. It looked very black in the dark of the silent, sleeping house.

I am not seeing this. This is not real. This is just a vision... or a byproduct of them. He closed his eyes, counted to three, and opened them, but the blood was still there. He could even smell it, a thick, meaty, slightly rotten odor that coated his throat.

His gaze moved to the stairs, and the bottom dropped out of his stomach. There was blood there, too—it trailed in a thin, uneven line from the puddle at his feet all the way up to the second floor.

Oh, God, he thought, the panic in his gut clawing its way up his throat. *Is that Sylvia's blood?*

He bolted to the stairs and took them two and three at a time. When he reached the landing, he saw that the trail of blood trickled down the hall to his and Sylvia's bedroom. His heart tightened in his chest.

Please let her be okay...please let her be okay....

He skirted the blood and dove headlong into the stifling dark of the bedroom. It was thick in there, the darkness—almost too thick to breathe or think, and definitely too thick to see anything more than a silhouetted form lying on the bed.

"Sylvia?" His voice came out more as a whisper than a word. As he crossed the room to the bed, the shadows around him, inky and amorphous, seemed to swallow all sound.

He bent over her form and called her name again, his mouth

close to her ear, and reached toward her shoulder to wake her.

His hand went through the form on the bed, sinking into a dampness that made him scream.

His hand must have reached for the light without his thinking about it, because the room was suddenly flooded from the bedside table lamp, and Sylvia, looking startled and sleepy but otherwise okay and unharmed, sat upright in the bed.

"Oh my God, Tim! What's wrong?"

"I...I—" His wild gaze scanned the room. What had just happened to him? What was going on? There was no blood there—not on the bed, nor the floor, nor even in what he could see of the hallway. He was baffled. Had it really been another vision, so close on the heels of the last two? If so, these were so different than any he'd had before. These were...intrusive, disrupting his reality. For the first time in decades, he felt genuinely scared of them.

"I thought—I thought I saw blood and—and my hand went through you and...*Christ*."

She searched his face. Seeming to find real fear there, she pulled him gently into a hug. He buried his face gratefully in her hair, inhaling the scent of her, holding on tightly.

"What happened tonight?" she asked softly in his ear.

He spent the next forty-five minutes telling her or trying to tell her. There was so much that made no sense, so much that seemed to be slipping away with the night. He tried to make her understand about the little girl in the club, how he had gazed into a void inside her and nothing had made much sense from that point. He told her about the drive home and the blood and how he couldn't get those twisted shapes of teenagers out of his head. The sun had come up by the time he was finished, its early-morning rays streaming through the windows, but she sat and listened, taking it all in without comment or judgment. He wasn't sure whether she believed his night was a string of real events or hallucinations, but if Tim were to be honest with himself, it was hard for him to tell, either, in the more veritable light of day. He was so, so tired. So tired.

Once his story and his body had wound down, she patted his side of the bed and pulled back the covers, murmuring that they'd sort it all out after some rest. At that moment, nothing sounded better to him. He fell into bed beside her, holding her close until he fell into a deep sleep.

Tim woke up to the alarm going off. The loud buzzing seemed to be coming from his head, a remnant of a dream already dissipating.

He frowned before he even opened his eyes. Stupid alarm shouldn't be going off—it was set for Monday through Friday to get him up for work during the school year, and he hadn't gotten around to resetting it. That shouldn't have mattered, though. It was Saturday.

He smacked at the OFF button and cracked an eye open to glare at it without really registering what the blue LED lines were telling him about day, time, and temperature.

He sank back into the dark behind his eyelids, sleep once again enshrouding him until a stronger, late-morning sunshine fell on him from the window. He felt better; Sylvia was good to have let him sleep so long. She must have seen he needed it. He rolled over and opened his eyes.

The digital clock cheerfully offered its blue-lit information again: the time: 10:43 a.m., the day: Friday, the temperature: 76 degrees.

Tim made a face. That day was wrong, though it explained why the alarm had gone off. He got up, yawning, and searched the little black box for a way to change the settings. No button made itself immediately apparent to him, so he replaced the clock and made his way down to the kitchen.

"Good morning, handsome," Sylvia said over her pan of frying eggs. She didn't turn around but he could hear the cheerful smile in her voice. He came up behind her and slipped his arms around her, kissing her cheek. "Good morning, beautiful. Thanks for letting me sleep. I needed it."

"Sure," she said. "I'm surprised you were able to sleep so late, but hey, if you did, it must be your body's way of telling you that you needed it, right?"

"I'd say so, after last night," Tim said.

Sylvia turned around then, a playful smile on her face. "All our binge-watching took a lot out of you, did it?"

Tim cocked his head to the side, confused. "No, I meant… the club…Charlie, remember? I went out to Club 138 because of the vision I had?"

Now it was Sylvia's turn to look confused. "Baby, you were here all night last night. We watched *The Shield*, remember?"

Tim shook his head slowly. "Uh, no, that was Thursday night. Syl, don't you remember me telling you everything that happened? The club? The little girl? The blood in the hallway?"

Sylvia frowned at him. "Last night was Thursday night, hon. Today is Friday. And what are you talking about? What blood?"

"Wait…." Flustered, Tim glanced at the calendar on the fridge. Sylvia was a stickler for making sure the days were crossed off. He had teased her once about being a little obsessive when it came to making sure those neat little X's ticked off the passing days before she went to bed, but she claimed it gave her a sense of order, a progression of the tidier schedules of life. It made her feel like things were finished for the day and she could relax and go to bed. And sure enough, all the days were crossed off—right up until Thursday. Friday was a blank white square.

"That can't be right," he muttered, wandering over to the fridge. He touched the white box of Friday as if he couldn't quite believe it was there. He had seen her mark off Thursday night, but that had been *two* nights ago. He'd assumed Friday had been similarly dispatched after he'd left for the club. Yet there was no ink smudge, no indentation in the calendar paper, nothing at all to indicate it had been touched.

He turned to her, taking in the concerned expression on her face before saying, "This can't be right…it doesn't make sense. I lost a whole day. Or gained it back. Or something."

"Honey, are you all right?"

He nodded absently, his attention returning to the calendar.

"Maybe you dreamed it? It sounds pretty vivid. Maybe it was a vision inside a dream? Do you do that? Does it ever happen that way?"

Her words fell like a light rain on his head but he wasn't

taking them in. There had been a massacre, for God's sake. It had to be in the paper. He turned to the kitchen table and saw it lying there next to the cup of coffee she'd poured for him, and he snatched it up, scrutinizing the first page. The date indicated that it was indeed Friday, but there was no mention of the mass murder at Club 138. He clicked his tongue in disbelief. There was nothing—absolutely nothing. He leafed through the pages, scanning each carefully, but there wasn't a single inch of ink devoted to what he had witnessed the night before. He let the paper fall from his hand.

"Honey?" Behind him, Sylvia touched his shoulder. Her voice had that tone that meant she was concerned but trying not to bombard him with questions, a tone she usually reserved for just before, after, or during one of his visions.

Tim turned to her. "It's Friday? You're sure? You're not messing with me?"

"Of course not," she said gently. "I'm not even sure what's going on."

Tim shook his head. "Me neither. Look, something happened, I guess it was last night some time. It's very confusing. I have to sort this out, get my head right. I don't know if I had a really strong vision or dream or what, but...but I need to check a few things out and maybe try to make sense of things. Then I'll try to explain it. Okay?"

Sylvia nodded. Tim wondered sometimes where she got those seemingly endless reserves of patience and understanding. "Sure, sure. Go ahead and do what you have to."

He kissed her cheek and left her standing in the kitchen, probably wondering if his psychic ability had finally caused the fissures in his mind to split wide open and all his reason and sanity to tumble into them. He wasn't so sure something very much like that hadn't happened. He felt dizzy and a little sick around the edges, like he'd taken one too many turns on a roller coaster. He didn't think it was just him that was off-kilter, though. Something was very wrong, and if those nagging suspicions crawling up out of those mind-fissures were correct, then he wasn't the only one who'd have reason to worry.

Tim had showered and shaved and was in the car by quarter to one, and the first place he drove to was Club 138. Part of him wasn't really surprised to find no police presence and no crime scene tape blocking off the empty parking lot. He parked in the lot and got out, watching the building for a moment as if something might happen—the horrors of the night before maybe leaking out the windows. It was quiet, though, lazing in the mid-day while its patrons slept off the night before or readied themselves for the night to come.

He made his way to the spot where he'd seen the twins and Pete, or thought he'd seen them. Had he? He would have sworn on a stack of Bibles that he had. Shaking his head, he turned the corner. He could remember so much vivid detail about the crowd of terrified teens that had stood shivering in that street. How could that have been a vision? They were never so clear, so complete, or so chronological. It hadn't been a flash of premonition, like what had served to motivate him to find Charlie. It was a memory, a clear one.

And yet there was no crime scene tape across the front door, either. What he did find was a hastily handwritten sign that indicated the club would be closed that weekend and would re-open the following Friday. Tim guessed it was possible that if it all was a vision of what was to be, that it didn't necessarily have to be that night…or even that club. But what then? Was he supposed to check a bunch of local clubs for a bunch of Fridays in a row until something horrible happened? That was crazy.

Crazy like a little girl with a void inside a mouth inside a stomach.

On a whim, he tried the door. It was locked, as it ought to have been. He tried to peer through the window to the right of the door, but other than some chairs overturned on tables and that scuffed bar, there wasn't too much to see in the gloomy interior.

He backed out into the street where he could have sworn he'd stood less than twenty-four hours before and took the building in. There was nothing he could see that indicated the previous night had ever even happened.

So…it was a vision, then, a dream-vision maybe—a vivid,

detailed, realistic one, but a dream all the same. And that was all. No dead children-things, no mangled bodies, no real danger or—

His gaze happened to fall on the bulletin board outside the club then, and a small black-and-white photo arrested his attention. He walked closer to it, an iciness in his stomach spreading quickly to his extremities. It was a picture of a little girl of about nine, with long, straight, light-colored hair. She appeared to be standing in a back yard or park—somewhere grassy, with swings and a slide—and she was holding a puppy. The caption above the picture claimed she was MISSING SINCE JUNE 4 and the details beneath gave her height, weight, hair color, and eye color, as well as the fact that she was last seen walking home from school.

The sadness that missing children's posters ignited in him was compounded into horror as he realized he recognized her, though in this picture, she seemed healthy, full of natural vibrancy and life. In this picture, her eyes were not obsidian black, nor did her soft, light skin have the spider-webbing of poisonous little veins. She wore a T-shirt with flowers on it and jeans instead of the old-fashioned church-lady hat and jumper. In this picture, she was very much alive.

Miss Circle.

The thought popped into his head with such a suddenness that it jarred him. It didn't have the texture of his thoughts at all. It wasn't a name, and certainly not this girl's name which, according to the poster, was Karen Eberley. He had to acknowledge, though, that for reasons he hadn't quite consciously worked out, he'd come to think of the little wraith he'd seen in the club as Miss Circle.

His mouth suddenly felt very dry, almost crackling. Karen Eberley. Miss Circle. How could the two be connected? Every theory he concocted sounded insane. Children went missing— it was a tragic and horrible thing, but it happened. They were either recovered alive or their bodies were found. They did not slip into other dimensions, despite what that bookstore guy had said about his daughter in the papers a while back. They did not become monsters capable of mangling a club full of teenagers.

So how to explain the striking similarities? Coincidence? Dopplegängers? He reached for the poster and tore it down, stuffing it into the pocket of his jeans. If anything about last night had been real, then he knew one person who would recognize the girl in the picture, too.

He had to find Charlie Bentner.

FOUR

Tim returned home to an empty house; his wife had gone off to work but had left a note on the Post-it pad which they kept by the house phone. It simply read: *Gone to work. Call if you need me. Love you.* He felt a pang of guilt along with love for Sylvia, who put up with so much not knowing, so much confusion just to support him and his "gift." He supposed she'd seen enough over the years to believe in it, and that she knew him well enough to know what kind of faith he put into it, but he was grateful all the same for her understanding. It was strong with him, that ability to connect however briefly to other planes of existence, though it had been stronger in his aunt and especially his grandmother, who in her day, had run a tidy little side business dispensing advice and occasional herbal remedies to the neighbors. With Tim, though, it was never an ability he had managed to refine to that degree, perhaps because it was so erratic. To him, it felt sometimes like he was trying to juggle half-drugged, hungry dreams.

He was able to find the Bentners' address through Google on his phone. It was disturbingly easy, and Tim made a mental note to remind his classes next year about the dangers of posting too much personal information online. Jotting the address down on a pad of his own, he tore the sheet loose and stuffed it in his pocket alongside the missing poster for Karen Eberley.

He paused in the front hallway, car keys in his hand. There was a folded newspaper on the front hall table by the door. On the side facing up was a picture of a smiling boy of about eight in a Little League uniform. The caption above the photo read: HUNT FOR MISSING BOY CONTINUES.

It was sheer impulse that drove him to tear the article free and stuff it into his pocket along with the other crumpled papers. Or maybe it was instinct; some part of Tim believed that it was possible that somehow the missing boy and the missing Karen Eberley had something to do with the girl-thing in the club and this whole reversed day. He wasn't sure what the connection was, exactly, but couldn't shake the feeling that it was only part of something bigger.

He jogged down the front steps and had almost made it to the driver's side of his car when he saw a little boy standing in the middle of the street a few feet away from Tim's driveway. His small hands were shoved into his pockets and his head was slightly tilted, like he found Tim an item of curiosity. Tim's first instinct was to ask if he was okay and had even gotten so far as opening his mouth...but then he closed it, stunned into silence.

It was Tim's little brother, Kyle.

The structure of the facial features was identical; there was no doubting that. The age...that was how Tim remembered his ten-year-old brother. However, there was a number of differences that made the child in the street far more similar to the girl at the club. For one thing, there was something surreal, almost wavering about the little form, like Tim was seeing him through a heat-haze. The skin was the same pale gray, actually, as the black-and-white photo of the newspaper. The overall effect struck Tim as being like a mirage or a hallucination, the boy peeled right off a photo and pasted over Tim's reality. Unlike in his memories, the colorless hair was combed in a 1940s part-and-sweep to the side, which might have lent an aspect of cherubic innocence to the little figure if not for that baleful glare beneath. The eyes were enveloped in black, like shark eyes, and there was such a malevolence in them that it overshadowed the little nose, bony cheeks, and grimly set mouth. The clothes were anachronistic as well, holdovers from a bygone era of knickers and suspenders.

Then the boy opened his mouth, and it kept opening. It stretched impossibly wide, his chin descending past the collarbone, then past the skinny chest, unhinging like a snake to drop toward the navel. A spiral of transparent teeth, like jagged shards of glass, circled just beneath those stretched-too-thin lips and swirled down into the darkness of its throat. The skin of the face had begun to marble with that same vein poison as the girl in the club.

Tim fought the urge to scream. Instead, he fumbled with the keys at the car door's lock, jabbing them at the metal until finally the right key sank in and he could turn it and open the door.

The boy advanced toward him, and Tim cried out. That gaping maw made no sound, but Tim imagined that there was a rushing sound like waves crashing in an ocean or machines turning over and over, a dull roar of eons of hate from that same limitless internal space as the one the girl from the club carried in her stomach.

Tim slipped into the driver's seat and slammed the door, his attention drawn immediately to the rear view as he shoved the key in the ignition.

The boy was gone. The engine came to life—a safe, familiar kind of roar—but panic gripped Tim by the throat. God, where was it, that horrible little mummer masquerading as a boy-thing? Where had—

(*Mr. Triangle*)

—gone with that gaping mouth? Was it behind the car? If so, he'd crush it beneath the wheels. He threw the car into Reverse and was about to floor the gas pedal when a heavy thump on the driver-side window made him jump, screaming into the confines of his car. He turned and saw the boy-creature standing just outside, its jaw back in place but that same obsidian-eyed stare boring into him. The boy raised one pale little finger and traced a triangle on the window, leaving as he did so a thin trail of bright red blood.

Tim stomped on the gas and the car jerked backwards, away from those eyes and that finger and out into the street. He threw it into Drive and the car lurched forward. Tim switched to the brake for a moment, only so he could check the driveway, but he was pretty sure it wasn't a vision or hallucination this time, either. He felt his heart tighten in his chest.

The boy stood on the sidewalk in front of his house, waving, and blood *(not its blood, but someone else's,* Tim's mind insisted) dripped from the curling fingers. Then it wavered and grew transparent, and winked out of view.

Tim switched to the gas again and tore off, heading for Charlie Bentner's place.

The home of Rick and Jodi Bentner at 1158 Corvus Street was at the end of town generally considered to be sparser, blander, and cheaper. The whole neighborhood in which Corvus Street was nestled reflected the exhaustion of its owners, with the corners of things always breaking loose or dripping or clogging where they shouldn't. There was a fade to these houses, much like the people who lived in them, born of the weighty knowledge that this was as good as life was going to get, and it wasn't so great.

The Bentner house was no different. A chipped tan bi-level with sad, sagging gray windows and a porch on the verge of rot, it seemed to sigh at Tim's approach, as if used to strangers showing up at all odd hours, and making trouble for someone within its confines. The lawn needed a trim, but other Saturday and Sunday obligations evidently had muscled their way ahead of the grass on the priorities line. The mailbox leaned a little to the left on the post by the curb, and Tim found a small smile crept over his face as he imagined Charlie and his friends taking a whack at it with sticks or baseball bats, their mostly innocent childhood attempt at rebalancing the universe.

Charlie's car slouched in the driveway, its right front bumper a little loose. A peeling sticker in the back window declared his admiration for the Misfits.

Tim parked in front of the house and cut the engine. Likely, Charlie would be in there alone, or as good as alone; Tim had been counting on that. He didn't need the extra hassle of trying to circumnavigate Charlie's parents. If it really was Friday and not Saturday, then Rick Bentner would be at work. Charlie had never been particularly forthcoming about his parents (they were not a close-knit, "sit-down dinner at six" kind of family), but he had always seemed to admire at the very least the work ethic of his father, who worked two jobs and a well-over-40-hour work week. His mother, if town rumor were to be believed, would be passed out on the couch, or working her way there.

Tim sat in the car, hesitant. What if Charlie didn't remember? Where did that leave Tim? He supposed that selfishly, he wanted to believe Charlie was in this mess with him because it spoke to his own sanity. His grandmother had managed tolerably well, even into old age with the first signs of senility setting in, but his aunt hadn't had an easy time of things. Her "gift" had finally driven her crazy, to the point where there was little if any difference in her mind between past, present, and future, reality and visions, or dreams and everyday life. Tim was secretly terrified of that happening to him, in the deepest parts of his brain where even he didn't dare to go consciously. This whole time-hiccup had really thrown him for a loop, and he didn't know where to go from there if it turned out Charlie had no idea about the girl-thing in the club or anything else.

Eventually, though, an old lady giving him the suspicious eye as she passed walking her dog and the notion that nothing would be solved sitting behind the wheel of his car spurred him to action. He got out and made his way up the cracked driveway to the front door.

He was about to knock when the door opened, startling him. The face staring back at him was Charlie's, but it was in bad shape. Exhaustion hung in dark bags beneath eyes otherwise wide and shining with nervous energy. There was a bruise on his left cheek and another on his jaw, and although Tim could only see a sliver of Charlie, there appeared to be bruises on the boy's neck as well.

"Charlie? What the hell happened to you?"

"Jenks." Charlie opened the door just enough to reach out and pull Tim in by the sleeve before quickly closing the door behind them.

The hallway was small and dark and smelled faintly like cigarette smoke. Charlie, hugging himself tightly and shifting his weight from foot to foot, chewed on a fingernail then waved Tim to follow him. He led Tim to the kitchen, which, even when Charlie flicked on the light, was not much cheerier than any other part of the house Tim had seen. Charlie sank into one of the chairs and Tim sat across from him, noticing even more bruises on the boy's arms.

"You look—"

"They came here this morning," the boy said, his eyes darting nervously to the doorway and back.

"Who came? Who did this to you?"

"The girl from the club, the thing with the universe in her stomach. That…that was last night, wasn't it?"

He remembered. Tim breathed an inward sigh of relief for himself. He nodded slowly. "I'd swear to it, though everyone else seems pretty sure yesterday never happened at all."

"I know. I know." Charlie chewed on his nail again for a moment, then said, "But it did, right? Because I remember, and even though I called Mike and he said everyone's fine and all of the guys swear we haven't been to the club in weeks, I fucking remember. That thing, that little girl thing or whatever—I remember her."

"Yes, me too."

"Well, she followed me. She came with uh, I dunno, like, another little girl-thing, and—" He stopped suddenly, eyes growing wide again. "Did you hear that?"

Tim paused before shaking his head. "I didn't hear—"

"They came this morning," Charlie repeated. Those things that hurt all those people at the club. They…hit me, but without touching me. I think they might have sprained my wrist." He indicated the wrist that he had been keeping tucked close to his ribs, and it did look to Tim to be reddish and a little swollen.

"Jesus, Charlie. I'm sorry." Tim reached out to check the boy's wrist but Charlie pulled away, wrapping it around his ribs again. It wasn't a gesture of rejection so much as absentmindedness, Tim gauged from the boy's expression. Charlie seemed only half with him. Tim assumed shock and lack of sleep were taking their toll. "Charlie, I need you to tell me everything that happened."

The boy drummed the fingers of his good hand, the one with the chewed nails, on the table. "Well, I had gotten home from the club, right? And my parents were asleep, so I went up to my room and got ready for bed. I guess I was still amped up from the club shit, so I turned on the TV and…nothing. Nothing on the news, nothing on the web when I looked, and none of the guys were answering their phones. I couldn't find nothing—"

"Anything," Tim corrected by force of habit, then, waved it off and said, "Sorry. Go on."

"I couldn't find anything anywhere, so I shut off the light and figured I'd try to just go to sleep, you know? Just block it all out for the night and try to have a few hours of normal sleep. And…I dunno, maybe I slept a little, though it didn't feel like it. I remember at one point I looked out the window and the sky was lighter, but my room was still dark.

"And then I heard giggling.

"I didn't even have to turn the light on, Jenks. They fucking glowed in the dark, and it took jamming my fist in my mouth not to scream like a little girl."

He chuckled then, as if the thought of screaming like a little girl was ironic. "I jumped out of bed and then flung on the light and I saw there were two of them, both in those weird clothes with their black eyes and gray skin. They wavered a little when I turned on the light, as if…I dunno, readjusting. They were sitting on top of my dresser. They smiled at each other and then they smiled at me, and I swear, Jenks, they wanted to kill me. They wanted to break all my bones just like those people at the club. But they settled for beating the shit out of me instead.

"They never left the dresser, that's the crazy part. They just sat there tracing shapes in the air like they were drawing on a driveway with chalk or something, and then I'd get this bolt of pain like I'd been sucker-punched. And any time I tried to cross the room toward them, you know, to like, stop them, they just traced their shapes and *bam!* Down I'd go."

"Did they say anything to you?"

Charlie looked away. "They didn't talk, exactly. At least, not with their mouths. But I could hear them all the same— maybe in my head or something. I'm not sure. I didn't get much. Something about being summoned, about pavers and bone-sigils and breaths."

"That doesn't make any sense," Tim murmured, more to himself than Charlie. Nevertheless, the boy looked up helplessly.

"I told you I didn't get much. They were beating me up, remember? Something...something about them being summoned, that the sigils carved on the bones brought them. That's it. That's what they said. They used a word—I can't remember it now, but I think it was the word they used to mean others like them. And they said they were pavers of the way for their brethren."

Tim frowned. "They said they were summoned? Someone brought them here?"

"I guess." Charlie shrugged.

"Did they say anything else?"

"They told me it wasn't time to kill me yet," Charlie's voice broke, "because I would bring the summoners. What does that mean, Jenks? I don't know who summoned them! All I wanted was to talk to my girl! I don't even know how I got involved in this." He turned his head, mashing the fist of his good hand into his eyes to stop the tears.

When he'd composed himself a little, he added, "Oh, and they told me that Kyle is sleeping at the bottom of the sunbeam, whatever that's supposed to mean."

Tim felt his stomach drop out, and a coldness spread all over beneath his skin. "Who?"

"Kyle, I think? Yeah, I'm pretty sure they said Kyle. They told me to tell you. They know your name, Mr. Jenkins."

"Charlie," Tim said, leaning in anxiously, "I need you to be more than pretty sure."

Charlie, looking confused, said, "Yeah. Yeah, it was Kyle. Why?"

Tim sighed. "It's a long story. Even my wife doesn't know all the details." He pulled out the Missing poster and laid it on the table, followed by the newspaper article, then added, "Kyle was my little brother."

FIVE

Tim and Kyle Jenkins had been going to Sunbeam Lake every summer for as long as they could remember. For Tim, the memories were like landscape paintings in his mind's eye: rich, dark-green velvety patches of shadowed woods sponged over with lighter greens and golds rustling in warm winds. Tall grasses reached over from their banks to graze streams as they burbled along to a lake of slate gray with slips of lighter blue and white dancing on its surface. There were Rockwellian white fishing boats and small, nondescript wooden buildings for hikers and campers. There was a dock several feet out toward the center of the lake whose dark-green paint had faded summers ago, and yet still served as the goal and marker for many a swimming challenge. There were picnics with the first sips of beer and dogs barking and chasing Frisbees and children shouting. There were ten-speed bikes with cards clipped to the spokes and pink sunsets and lightning bugs and fireworks. Those yearly week-long vacations to Sunbeam Lake were the highlights of Tim's year, a time to be a boy and explore the world with innocence and awe, imagination, and enthusiasm.

That is, until the summer Tim was twelve.

The week had been unseasonably rainy, leaving the Jenkins boys a little stir-crazy. There were only so many games of Go Fish or Old Maid one could play, and despite the weather, only so much time allowed for Atari or watching taped movies on the VCR. Tim had been itching to go out, even if it meant playing in the rain and the mud. By late Thursday, the downpour had stopped but everything was still too soggy to enjoy. It wasn't until Friday morning that Tim was finally, thankfully, able to fling open the front door of the little cabin and run out into sunshine, his little brother close behind.

They had been close, the brothers, close enough to play together despite their two-year age difference. They squabbled occasionally, as brothers do, arguing who got to be Luke and who got to be Han Solo, bickering about boundary lines and the trajectories of imaginary bullets, but for the most part, it was the two of them against pirates, supervillains, monsters, Decepticons, the Empire, Cobra Command, and countless other plagues on justice and goodness.

They had been in the process of formulating an escape from a deadly jungle planet, in fact, when they came upon the silvery mass in the woods.

"What the hell is that?" Using swear words, even the small ones, was an intoxicating new power for Kyle, a toe-dip into the forbidden and adult. It was understood that when the brothers were together, language was a tattle-free thing to be shared and explored like any other alien world.

"Damned if I know," Tim said. They had made their way through a particularly deadly group of man-eating alien ferns, and Tim had stumbled a little on the dirt path. The toe of his sneaker had slid into a gelatinous mass of silver shaped like a tadpole. When he drew his foot away, the mass had quivered and issued a sound like a moan, which could have just been wind over the water.

Crouching down, Tim picked up a stick and poked at it. Up close, Tim could see threads of red like tiny veins all throughout the silver, and a yolk-like part that reminded him of a filmy eye. Kyle crouched down next to him.

"Think it's like, an animal or something?"

"No way. Never seen an animal like that."

"Well, it's moving. Look—it's crawling up the stick."

And so it was. A tendril of the silver was oozing upward toward his hand. Tim had a moment of revulsion at the thought of that silvery stuff touching his fingers and was about to drop the stick when the tendril snapped it in half. The part of the stick submerged in the mass began to smoke and then dissolve, and the red veins all around it pulsed as if happy to be fed. The boys, wide-eyed, scooted backward away from it. They both kept their eyes fixed on it, though. It was shaking visibly and seemed to be both increasing in size and moving toward them.

"Tim...?" Kyle sounded like he was trying very hard not to be afraid.

"Just back away, Kyle. Slowly. Just back away." Tim scrambled to his feet, yanking his brother up by the T-shirt. The silvery thing, meanwhile, began to rise, pulling itself into a head and shoulders. The boys screamed, startling a flock of birds in the tree above them and sending them into flight. Tim remembered wishing he could fly, then, too, to get away from the thing resolving itself into a vaguely humanoid form.

"Run!" he shouted to his brother. His feet, he felt sure, would never be fast enough to outrun it. Kyle hesitated, perhaps also worried that his feet weren't up to the task, and Tim barked the order again.

Tim didn't remember picking up a bigger, sharper stick and plunging it through the head-shaped part of the mass, right through that egg-yolk eye of filmy gray. The mass wailed, a shrill and terrible sound that hurt his ears. He turned to run. Kyle had gone on ahead; Tim thought he saw a glimpse of his brother's T-shirt before it disappeared behind a tree. Tim took off. He allowed himself to feel some relief in knowing his brother had gotten away, but it was eclipsed by horror pressing down on his back; he didn't dare turn around, but he could hear it—a wet, rhythmic, smooching sound like footsteps, moving surprisingly fast.

Tim supposed it was adrenaline that had kept his feet flying over a hundred things that should have tripped him, twisted his ankle, and sent him rolling back into the shuddering silver nightmare closing the distance behind him. And he was sure the thing was gaining on him, because that horrible wet sloshing sounded closer, mere steps behind him now. His chest burned, and it felt like a bomb was about to go off where his heart was. His legs ached and although he didn't feel it then, he'd discover later a myriad of little scratches from tiny twigs and thorns.

He wasn't going to make it. The silver blob was going to catch him, ooze over him, dissolve him into the tiny red threads....

Tim was breathing too hard to scream.

When he finally broke free of the woods and into the rolling lawn of the cabin's back yard, relief flooded his body with heat.

Tears streamed down his cheeks.

His mother was reading a book in a lawn chair and had looked up just as he collapsed into her lap.

"Whoa. Whoa, baby. What's the matter? What happened? Where's your brother?"

Tim was crying too hard to talk; when the crying managed to subside to heaving breaths and then little shivers, he spilled the whole story about playing, finding the silvery thing in the woods, poking it, telling Kyle to run as it got bigger and bigger....

The whole time, he kept shooting terrified glances at the woods from which he'd come, convinced that the thing would emerge any minute, larger from maybe having engulfed and dissolved birds or squirrels or even a deer.

Somewhere during the recounting of his story, Tim's father had emerged from the cabin as well. Both his parents remained quiet for a time, taking in his story and his insistence, even though there were no remarks to the contrary, that he was telling the truth about all of it. When he finally paused long enough to take a breath, though, they repeated the one question Tim's story didn't answer.

"Son, it's okay. It's okay. We've got you now. You're safe. But honey, where's your brother? Where's Kyle?"

It took a moment for the question to penetrate Tim's haze of adrenaline, but when it did, a deep sense of dread welled up inside him. "Isn't—didn't he come back here? He was ahead of me! I saw him! I saw him running!"

It was then that his parents panicked.

The rest of that weekend, particularly that Friday night, was a blur. There were cops and dogs and flashlights searching the woods with Mr. Jenkins. Mrs. Olliphant, the nice lady from next door who sometimes made them cookies, sat with his mom and let her cry until her eyes were red.

The prevailing theory of police and neighbors was that something had happened out on the forest trail, and it had scared Tim's little brother so badly that the younger boy had gone off somewhere in the woods to hide. Whether that something was a scenario that Tim himself created or some natural phenomenon that had scared both the boys to tears was debated in that upper air space of hushed voices spoken over children's heads.

The weekend had extended another week and a half as search parties scoured the woods. There had been no sign of the silvery mass Tim described. There had been no sign of Kyle, either. Both, it seemed, had vanished as if neither had existed at all.

None of the police or neighbors or townsfolk who came out to help that night or at any time after ever blamed Tim to his face, and no one called into question any part of his story, but Tim felt the doubt and the questions lurking behind their comforting and reassuring eyes and smiles. They were trying to be nice, because obviously something had scared Tim and his brother very badly, but a silver gelatin person with one eye that could dissolve solid objects upon touch? Well, Tim had always had an active imagination, as many boys did. He had been told countless times to keep those stories to himself and not terrorize his little brother or tell tales outside of the family. And after his brother's disappearance and the start of the terrible headaches, the stories just got wilder, and even if sometimes parts of them came true, it was coincidence, and could you blame the poor boy, needing something to hold on to, something to make him feel less powerless....

Tim had once pointed out that his estranged aunt and his dearly departed grandmother would have believed him, that maybe Aunt Lucy could help find Kyle and tell them what the silver thing had been, but that had just made his mother cry so hard and his father shout so loudly that Tim had never brought it up again.

When the Jenkins family, one member short, could finally be convinced to leave the cabin and go back home to their fall and winter lives, it had broken his mother's spirit. It was like some of her substance had been carved out of her, and until her death a few decades later, she had been a shadow against the walls of the family home, there but not there. Tim's father, a practical man, continued with annual trips to the cabin wherein he resumed his search for some sign of his little boy. His annual failure to find Kyle wore on his face and his stature.

If they resented Tim for losing Kyle or for somehow failing to protect him, they never said, but they didn't need to. Tim did enough of that for all three of them. Tim had had the occasional strange dream before, but after Kyle's disappearance, they became waking visions, almost unbearably strong. High school had been tough, a series of cut classes and self-medication and suspensions. It was not lost on Tim that guys like Charlie Bentner struck a nerve with him. For God's sake, they were him—a him that he'd left behind simply because to hold on would have left him as lost as Kyle, and maybe just as dead.

The year Tim left for college, his brother Kyle was declared legally dead in absentia. His parents buried an empty box and put a tombstone over it. There was no closure in it. Tim remembered feeling an almost unreasonable hatred for the stone, which, through no fault of its own, could never capture the life of the body it should have rested above, the ten years of brotherhood, of a bedroom of toys and clothes untouched in six years, of a voice and a footfall never to be heard again. A tombstone, with its name and dates and oversimplified phrase of BELOVED SON AND BROTHER could never do justice to Kyle, and Tim resented it for that.

It had taken some profound self-examination to understand that what Tim really resented was himself. All those glimpses of the future, all those precognitive dreams and visions, and never once had he been able to glean anything about the disappearance of his brother. What was the good in having any kind of psychic ability if the one useful thing he could do with it was withheld from him? He couldn't find Kyle, couldn't contribute any more to the understanding of what happened to him than that damned slab of rock over his grave.

But then he'd had the vision about Charlie, and something about the shapes, whatever they were, had struck him as familiar. The wail of the girl-thing in the club, the certainty that some gelatinous, silvery mass lay beneath the thin veneer of corpse-like childskin that covered those things…. And now the mention of Kyle and Sunbeam Lake. There was a connection somewhere, although what it was, or how Charlie fit into it, Tim couldn't figure out.

All he could ascertain, he concluded to Charlie at the kitchen table, was that the thing he had been running from in the woods, the thing that to be honest, he had never really stopped running from, had caught up to him. And he was sure it intended to engulf and dissolve both him and Charlie unless they could stop it.

"Okay," Charlie said quietly. "So what do we do next?"

SIX

The edges of the rip in the universe wavered and shimmered, catching and reforming shadows along the broken floor of the abandoned house as the setting sun slipped in all around it.

The house stood on the edge of a crumbling Revolutionary War cemetery, once a home to the caretaker and his family. Gaping holes yawned in the front porch floor. Splintering boards had been nailed over the empty frames where the front door and the windows had been, but sunlight still found its way in to illuminate the dancing motes in the air. The roof sagged beneath the weight of centuries, and the brick of the chimney formed a small pile of red rubble at its base. There weren't many houses like it anymore—colonial-era piles of kindling, more or less, held together by chance and the patriotic undercurrent of residents who saw fit to leave such things as historical landmarks, officially or unofficially. The house was one of the unofficial ones, but recognized as a thing which had always been, at least so far back as current residents could remember, and would be until nature took it apart again. There were signs all over the property that warned the occasional wanderer to KEEP OUT, as well as posted warnings that trespassers would be prosecuted by law.

The summoners had chosen the empty, dust-choked interior as the perfect place to open the rip. In truth, the interior was little more than one big room now anyway, not much of a fortress to keep things in or out, but then, the summoners hadn't really believed it would work anyway.

There had been no flash of light, no thunder and lightning, not even a small pop. The summoners had thought their experiment a failure. They'd lost interest by then, anyway; it had just been something to do on a Thursday night. They hadn't noticed the shimmer of the edges in the moonlight or felt the cool breeze of time and space shifting. Their reach had been far and their touch reckless, but they hadn't known. It had just felt good to go through the motions of getting one over on their teacher, Mr. Jenkins. It was, in fact, his bloody tissue that had made the spell work, but so far as the summoners knew, they had accomplished little more than a single-finger salute to his authority.

The shapes had not been expecting the rip, nor the snapping forward and backward in time that their crossing over would cause, but it amused them. Few things did anymore—not since the last rip, torn open by Hollowers passing through, had finally sealed up again.

And this particular summoning was serendipitous. One of their number had run into the owner of the blood, the one the summoners called Jenkins, once in that very dimension, in its past. Back then, the shapes hadn't understood what the dimension's air did to their natural forms. It hadn't gone well for poor Mr. Decagon…but his discovery, his acquisition, had changed everything. The shapes were not like the Hollowers, able to move freely between worlds at will. They needed partially physical vehicles to move about in. The bodies of child-things from this dimension's different times and places, partly devoured and partly assimilated, was just the right solution to their devolving and dissolving problems.

It had taken them awhile to understand dress; its nature and appearance changed so quickly in places with linear time. In the end, they'd chosen a style they liked and stuck with it.

It had taken them longer to break the communication barrier; the simple-minded creatures of the new dimension didn't understand the three-dimensional words of the Convergence. But that was okay. The shapes got by with a cobbled-together process of symbols and telepathy that seemed to convey their meaning. They had, in fact, grown to love a number of the rudimentary, flat symbols that constituted a means of communication in this new world. In particular, they were taken with what was thought of as basic geometry. This was in no small part due to the delightful discovery of the *names* of shapes, which cosmic coincidence showed them could actually be translated as three-dimensional words close to their own names and attributes in the language of the Convergence.

It had been Mr. Triangle who had first crossed over through the rip and brought back more bodies for them. Having been the only one to witness Mr. Decagon's dissolution, he'd gone back there to claim a body of his own; he'd known the right one immediately, he'd told them. Mr. Triangle had an uncanny sense of where and when to find bodies which he refused to explain to the others, even Miss Circle, and he told her mostly everything. Still, if Mr. Triangle wanted the important role of being sole body-finder, so be it. Even Mr. Hexagon didn't argue. The shapes were just excited to be moving again.

By the time the lot of them had new bodies to use, the rip had already begun to spread tendrils out into various locations all over the new dimension. The shapes had expected to emerge directly, but had been rerouted, in a manner of speaking, to another location. The time snap did not bother them, nor did the giddy uncertainty of dimensional travel, but the loud sounds in the place where they materialized were unbearable. They had sought to make those sounds stop, and had discovered, to their great pleasure, how easily and satisfyingly breakable the sound-making creatures were.

They had felt both the owner of the blood and the owner of the bones at that loud place; perhaps that was why they had been drawn there specifically. But neither were among the broken bodies. Miss Circle had caught a glimpse of them, had even tried to speak to them, but they had run. That was okay, too—all part of the great plan, Mr. Triangle said.

He told them what would come next. Miss Circle agreed with Mr. Triangle. Even Mr. Hexagon conceded that there was work to be done. They would work backward from the outer summoners to the inner ones. They would follow the great plan, and it would be fun.

"First, we find out what they are," Tim told Charlie. "Where they come from, how many there are, and how they can be killed. Then we kill them. All of them."

Charlie gave him a cynical look and shook his head. "And how do we do that?"

Tim shrugged and said, "You mentioned that they thought they had been summoned, right? And that they seemed pretty sure you know who those summoners are."

"They said that, yeah, but I don't know what they were talking about."

"Assuming they're, I don't know, some kind of demon," Tim went on, "then there was probably some ritual involved in calling them here. Did you dabble in some kind of black magic? Ouija board? That sort of thing?"

Charlie shook his head.

"Candles, sacrifices, anything?"

"Jenks, I'm not into that shit."

"I'm not judging you, Charlie. We just really need to get to the bottom of how they got here if we want to send them back to hell or wherever they came from."

The boy looked defensive. "How the fuck should I know? I don't—" He stopped, a realization dawning on his face like a small sunrise. "Scott."

"Scott...?"

Charlie nodded. "Scott. Scott Clinton, Jeremy's brother. He's into all that. I think maybe he might be who we're looking for."

Charlie's face grew pale. "Bones. They mentioned bones, and...oh my God, it's my fault."

Tim frowned. "What do you mean?"

Charlie took a deep breath and said, "When I was a kid, the doctors found that I was growing extra bones in my hand, like finger bones but in the wrong place. There were three of them, and I had surgery to have them removed. I was, like, five. Anyway, the doctors and my parents let me keep them, and you know, at five, that's like the coolest thing ever. I don't remember much about the surgery or recovery other than my hand still hurt a lot and was bandaged for weeks, but I remember thinking how cool it was to see those little bones in a jar." He smiled a little, but it faded quickly. "Jeremy came over a few weeks ago and asked about them, so I told him. He got all excited, like he'd never seen anything like it, and I just assumed it was...well, it's Jeremy, you know? Dude's got weird tastes.

"Anyway, I haven't seen the bones since. I guess I kinda figured right off that Jeremy swiped them. He's morbid like that—weird tastes, like I said. I was pissed, but, I dunno...it didn't seem like a thing worth getting into a fight with Jeremy about. He can be a real bastard if you piss him off. So I just let it go."

Tim was starting to make the connection. "And those things mentioned bones being used to summon them...."

"Right," Charlie said. "But Scott is dumber than a box of hair. He's no grand wizard or anything like that, just an asshole who's read the Satanic Bible and Anton LeVey's and Alister Crowley's shit. I can't imagine him being capable of...of summoning what we saw. Of those things."

"Maybe Scott isn't...but what about Jeremy?"

Charlie thought about that for a moment, then finally nodded.

"The question is," Tim continued, "why? Why would anyone want to call those terrible little monsters here?"

Charlie's face flushed. "They, uh, they're always talking about getting back at people. Beating the shit out of them, poisoning them, even putting death curses on them. Cops, store clerks...teachers. You."

Tim chuckled dryly, trying to hide his discomfort. He'd had students dislike him before, even hate him, though he'd always believed that it was more his being a symbol of authority that they hated rather than he himself. That anyone might so strenuously object to his being an authority figure as to want him dead unnerved him. Further, that someone wanted him dead so much as to cast a spell and set murderous dead children after him made him sick to his stomach. "Then why involve you? I thought you were their friend."

Charlie gave him a cynical look. "The Clinton brothers don't have friends. They have people afraid to be their enemies."

"That doesn't surprise me."

"I don't see how any of this is going to help. I mean, it's not like we can just go up to Scott and Jeremy and ask them to undo what they did."

"No," Tim said, rising from the table, "but we might find something useful where they performed this ritual. Would it have been at their house?"

"Doubt it," Charlie replied. "Someone's always yelling at someone there. And there are, like, a million little kids. No quiet, no privacy."

"So where?" Tim was getting impatient. He felt a headache coming on and suspected a vision was around its corner. The sooner they put together some information on these things, the better their chances of fighting them off.

"I don't know," Charlie said.

"Well, who would?"

"I guess maybe Mike Schuyler? I don't really—"

Tim grabbed Charlie's sleeve and pulled him to his feet. "Let's go, then. Call Mike and tell him we're coming. I don't think we have much time."

Tim could remember nothing else from the car ride over to Mike Schuyler's other than the vision. Charlie, looking terrified, had told Tim that he had seemed to faint and that the car started swerving. Charlie had reached for the wheel and managed to pull over as Tim let off the gas, and Charlie had thrown it into park, confused and scared, unsure whether to call 911 or run home or what. Tim had only been out a few minutes, but in those minutes, he had seen an old house with bloody walls being torn apart somewhere in deep space. He'd seen a little girl's eyes get really big before all the life of her had been sucked out, leaving a little dried husk. And he'd seen a terrible cloud of storms and eyes and teeth. His head pounded as the images began to fade, and he threw open the door to dry-heave over the street.

"I'm sorry," he told Charlie when he'd recovered enough to sit up and close the car door. He pulled away from the curb and continued on to Mike's house. "I—it happens to me sometimes like that. I see things, and then—"

"What did you see?" Charlie asked. He was still breathing hard, and Tim could see his hands were shaking. The poor kid had been through a lot already, and Tim didn't want to scare him any more than he had to. His hesitation seemed to worry Charlie even more, though, and the boy punched the dashboard. "Dammit, what did you see, Jenks?"

"A house," Tim blurted out. "An old house, abandoned, I think. And a storm. The rest is still a little hazy." It was partially true, what he'd told the boy—true enough to satisfy him.

Charlie nodded, exhaled his relief, and said, "Could that house be where they did, you know, the ritual?"

"Could be," Tim said. "Let's hope Mike knows." He pulled up in front of the house that Charlie indicated and parked. "Is it this one here on the right?"

"The blue one," Charlie said.

The Schuyler house was a two-story colonial, nothing like the house in his vision. It seemed well-kept and clean, so far as Tim could tell. There was a single car in the driveway, a beater that Tim assumed was Mike's car, but otherwise, the property suggested financial security and stability.

Tim and Charlie got out of the car and started up the driveway when the front door opened and Mike, looking pale and shaken, emerged from the house. He seemed only to barely register Tim's presence before turning to Charlie.

"Dude," Mike said, his voice soft, "he's dead."

Charlie and Tim exchanged looks.

"Who?" Charlie asked. "Who is?"

Mike shook his head. "Pete. All his bones are broken. Pete's dead."

SEVEN

"W-what the hell happened?" Charlie asked. With a shaking hand, he took the cigarette Mike offered and popped it between his lips as Mike lit it, then lit one of his own. Mike seemed then to remember Tim standing there, took the cigarette out of his mouth as if to hide it, realized he was on his own property, then clamped it between his teeth again. He held the pack out to Tim.

"No thanks," Tim replied.

"Mike," Charlie said, "tell us what happened to Pete."

"I—uh, I don't really know," Mike said with a shuddering breath. "It wasn't his dad—that was my first thought, too, but his mom said the bastard had gone out and didn't come back until this morning. She said he, uh, fell down the stairs, I think? Maybe. It was kinda hard to understand her with the crying and everything, and she said something about the way his bones were broken, that a fall couldn't do all that." He inhaled the cigarette smoke with a sharp *shhhzzz* sound, exhaled in jittery puffs, and continued. "I dunno, man. I dunno. Something's not right. Like, something's fucked up about this whole thing."

Charlie and Tim exchanged glances.

"When did it happen?" Charlie asked.

"He never did nothing to nobody, ya know?" Mike continued, as if he hadn't heard the question. "Pete was a good guy. He didn't deserve that. Big, loveable dumbass. For Chrissakes, he was only eighteen. That's too young to have all your bones broken, isn't it? Dude, even if he'd smoked a bowl, even if he'd smoked three…I mean, how many times has he gone down those fucking stairs stoned out of his mind and nothing happened? Stoned was like his normal. So why this time, huh?" Mike's voice was brittle, on the verge of breaking.

"When did it happen?" Charlie repeated.

"Last night. Late. His mom found him this morning." Mike looked at Charlie. "And like, I keep coming back to the last time we hung out, ya know? It was only last Thursday night, for God's sake. Drinking beers, listening to Jeremy and his fucking paranoid theories and Scott and his occult bullshit. You—wait, you weren't there that night. But Pete...." His voice trailed off, lost in the smoke of his next drag.

"Mike," Tim broke in gently, "about Thursday night, when you saw him...who were you with? Where were you?"

Mike looked at Tim as if he'd been asked to give up the combination to a safe. "Why?"

"Well," Charlie said, "it might explain what happened with Pete."

Mike looked genuinely confused. "How do you figure?" Then something seemed to occur to him. "Do you think someone, like, had it in for Pete? Like maybe someone pushed him down the stairs?"

Charlie looked uncomfortably at Tim.

"Let's not get carried away," Tim intervened. "If we knew what state of mind Pete was in Thursday night—you know, what was going on, what the vibe was like—it might help clarify what happened."

Mike nodded slowly. "Right. Right, okay." He finished the remainder of his cigarette, dropped it to the sidewalk, and crushed it under the toe of his sneaker. "Well, Jeremy and Scott came to pick me up that night. I remember my mom bitching because Scott's car radio was blasting Iron Maiden and Mom thought the neighbors were gonna get pissed off. So I got the hell outta there 'cause I didn't want her following me out into the street to cuss me out. I got in the car and Jeremy handed me a beer and I was like, 'What's the plan?' but at first they wouldn't tell me. Wouldn't say much of anything other than that they wanted to pick up Pete first, and that we were meeting some friends of Scott's for a little party." He shook his head and lit another cigarette. "Douchebags."

Tim leaned against the car. Charlie took another one of Mike's cigarettes and smoked in silence. Both waited for Mike to continue.

After several long drags on his own cigarette, he did.

"We picked up Pete at the park. His old man had been drinking and he had to split, so we met him at the usual spot. He seemed...fine. I dunno. He was just regular old Pete. Laid back. Stoned. Just Pete.

"Anyway, after we picked him up, we just drove around for a while. Jeremy and Scott still wouldn't tell us what was going on, but that's how those guys are sometimes. Charlie knows, right, brother? Pete and I weren't worried about it or anything, 'cause that's what they do. They can be assholes sometimes, always acting like they have these big, deep, dark secrets and have done all this crazy shit they can't talk about. Most of it's bullshit, I think. But hey, whatever, right? If that's what gets them off, good for them.

"So anyway, Pete and I are just drinking beers, having our own conversation in the back seat, and then all of a sudden, Jeremy shuts the music off and turns around to talk to us. He's got this weird look on his face. You know the look, Charlie. That look like he's getting ready to fuck with you."

Charlie nodded. Tim suspected from the boys' expression that it was a look they'd both seen far too often.

"He says, 'We're going to the cemetery.'

"So I said, 'I thought we were going to a party,' and he told us yeah, we were, but that the party was at the cemetery—that it had to be at the cemetery to do what he and Scott wanted to do. Of course, he didn't explain what that meant—neither of them did. I figured it was one of Scott's 'rituals.'" Mike made finger quotes around the word in the air. "Dude thinks he's some kind of satanist. Says he belongs to the Hand of the Black Stars or some shit."

"So, these guys took you to, what, a satanic ritual in the cemetery?" Tim asked. The more of the story Mike told, the worse Tim was beginning to feel. A pain had taken hold of the space behind his left eye, and he thought he felt, if not a vision, then some flash of dreadful insight coming on.

"Uh…yeah, I guess," Mike said. "I don't know too much about that shit, but it sure looked that way to me. When we rolled up to the cemetery, the one out on Covington, there was this little stone house."

"I know the one," Charlie said.

"It was all boarded up except for this one window—that was how we got in. I wish I'd stayed the hell home, though."

"What happened?" Charlie asked. He looked about as well as Tim was feeling. It was possible he knew, too—could sense it almost as strongly as Tim. Something very bad had happened in that little stone house.

"Well, the place was lit with candles everywhere and these weird chalk circles on the floor. I'd seen something like it in Scott's room once, but not nearly as complex. This one—it looked like it had taken hours to do. And there were all these dudes there in dark red robes standing around the outside of the circle. They didn't get too close to it, not at first. I figured they were Scott's weird friends. I don't think Scott's as seriously into the shit he talks about, but these guys…there were five of them, and they were scary dudes. Not physically big, you know? But scary. They had the coldest eyes, and when any one of them looked at me for too long, I could almost feel that cold, like when you're wearing wet clothes and it's windy.

"And then, I gotta tell you, I did get a little worried. I mean, part of me thought Scott and Jeremy were still fucking with us, trying to scare us, but I couldn't help wondering if maybe the dudes had finally snapped and were gonna sacrifice us or something. You read about shit like that sometimes, and don't figure on it ever happening to you 'til you're in a stone house in the middle of nowhere with a bunch of guys in robes with daggers and shit."

"And it didn't occur to you to leave?" Tim tried to reign in the judgmental quality that years and experience let creep into his voice, but from Mike's frown, he obviously hadn't been successful.

"No, man. I ain't no pussy. I wasn't gonna bolt just 'cause Scott's weird-ass friends wanted to chant some mumbo-jumbo and wave their dicks around a little."

Tim caught himself before he cautioned Mike on his language, and instead, waved for him to continue with the story.

"So there we were, the nine of us—apparently that was important, that exactly nine of us be there—and Jeremy pulls out this little bag of tiny bones. I thought they were animal bones at first—"

"They weren't," Charlie cut in. "They were mine. Surgery when I was a kid."

Mike nodded morosely. "Yeah, I know. He told us. Sorry, man. Sick fuck. I mean, I didn't believe him at first, but I sure as hell wouldn't put it past him to nick a dude's body parts.

"So then he takes out this bloody tissue. Says he snagged that from Mr. Jenkins's trash bin in school." He gave Tim a quick, guilty sideways glance and continued. "Said he needed blood and bones to 'call forth the shapes of the night.' Then he tossed the bones and the bloody tissue in the center of that circle on the floor, and I swear, when they hit the ground, I felt it. I knew that he wasn't bullshitting us, and that the bones and blood were human."

Mike stared at the lit tip of the cigarette as it began to burn the filter. "They started chanting something in this language that I've never heard before. Same two or three lines, over and over. Nine times, I think. I don't even know if it was a real language. Guess it was real enough to them, though."

"Did anything happen?" Tim asked.

Mike shrugged. "Hard to say. Nothing like you see in horror movies happened. But the air in the house was...different. Inhaling was like breathing in frost. And you know that feeling you get when you first wake up and aren't sure where you are? Or you're coming out of a blackout, and the world around you is a little different? It felt like that. Something had changed... but Pete and I seemed to be the only ones who noticed. One of the dudes in robes broke the silence by laughing and saying it hadn't worked. The guys took their robes off and they had regular clothes underneath. Then everyone sort of relaxed and started passing out beers and joints. They were all talking about the supernatural and alien worlds and dimensions, and Pete and I were sort of on the outside of it all, like we hadn't quite caught up in time to them. I just wanted out of there. I think I managed to choke down one beer before Pete and I called it a night and walked home. The whole time we walked, just the two of us in the dark, I kept hearing those words in my head. Pete tried to talk about other shit, but I think he was just as hung up on the words, too. And the thing is, nothing happened that we could see or hear, but we felt it. I did, and I know he did, because he didn't want to talk about it. So we just talked about bullshit. My last night hanging with Pete and we talked about Ali Marano's tits and the new Disturbed song he downloaded on iTunes. Fuck! I walked him to his door, Charlie. I was maybe the last person to see him. Maybe I could've...I don't know, stopped it somehow."

Charlie clapped a hand on Mike's shoulder. "You couldn't. You couldn't have known something like that would happen."

"Do you...uh, do you think he fell because of what those assholes did in that house?" Mike's voice was soft, so much so that the words seemed as ephemeral as the last streams of his cigarette smoke. "I mean, I don't see how, exactly, but maybe...I don't know...."

Charlie's and Tim's hesitation was answer enough for Mike. He grew very pale, and then asked, "So, does that mean I'm next?"

EIGHT

When Charlie and Tim had finished explaining what they'd seen and heard from their own night before, their Friday night, Mike looked dazed. He lit another cigarette with a shaking hand.

"Mike, this is very important," Tim broke in. "We need to know who the other five guys are."

"There were nine," Mike mumbled.

"Right," Tim replied patiently. "You, Pete, Jeremy, and... Scott, I believe you said. That's four of you right there. Who were the other five?"

"Oh, right," Mike said, and lit another cigarette. He looked up at Tim suddenly, then turned to Charlie. His expression was wild, like he was running through a flipbook of panicked thoughts behind his glassy eyes. "What's he doing here, man? Are you serious? Mr. Jenkins?"

Charlie glanced at Tim. "He knows, man. He's seen some shit. We're in trouble, dude, and ain't no one else gonna help us but him."

"I don't want help. I don't need it, and I don't need your trouble, okay? It was just some stupid thing we did. They did. I just stood there, really." Mike started to back away.

"Mike, wait," Tim began, but Mike shook his head.

"I didn't do nothing," he said, turning back to his house. "I didn't."

"Mike, please, for your own sake," Tim said, pushing off the car.

Mike flipped him off. "Screw you, Jenks. And screw you, too, Charlie. I don't want no part of this, okay? Just leave me alone."

Charlie clamped a hand on Mike's shoulder, and from the startled look on Mike's face, the grip must have been a strong one. Tim was surprised himself by the boy's set mouth and hard eyes and how he suddenly seemed much taller than Mike. For a moment, Tim considered intervening—he didn't like the sudden change in Charlie's demeanor—but he held off. Something told him to let the boy handle it.

"Mike, get a fucking grip," Charlie said quietly. "No one is blaming you or those other guys for Pete's death. It's not the cops you have to worry about. No one will ever prove Pete's death isn't an accident. But you and I and Mr. Jenkins know better, right? So you do need to talk to us, because you're in danger, just like Pete was. Just like Jenks and me are. And we can't fix this shit without information."

Mike shivered under his friend's touch. "What're you talking about?" he asked softly.

"It sounds like you already know," Charlie replied. "You said you felt it."

"It was the booze."

"Was it?" Charlie asked.

Mike didn't answer.

Charlie let go of his shoulder. "We weren't putting you on, Mike. Whatever the douchebag brothers were trying to call up in that old house, it worked. You have to trust me on this."

"No bullshit?"

"No bullshit," Charlie said.

Mike seemed to remember then that he had a cigarette, its forgotten ash nearly down to the filter. He flicked off the ash, took a long drag on what was left of his smoke, and then dropped it to the ground, forgotten.

"Bill Jacobsen was there," Mike said, exhaling a little stream of smoke. "Carl Austen. Pete, Jeremy, me, and Scott, like I said. George Clayton. I don't know the other guys. I think the one guy was named Jay. The other guy...I dunno, Al or Hal or something. Or maybe Bob. Who the fuck knows? I wasn't paying attention."

"Okay, good," Tim said in what he thought was an encouraging voice. "Good. Now, do you think you could show us this house?"

"Where the shit went down? The abandoned place? That house?"

"That would be the place," Tim said.

Mike considered this for a moment, then mashed the heel of his hand into his eyes and moaned. "Ahh, yeah. Yeah, I guess so. Is that, like, safe though? I don't wanna make nothing worse."

"I don't see how that's possible," Tim said.

Mike looked at him. "What, exactly, are we dealing with here? What did they summon?"

Tim opened his mouth to answer but found he had no words. He closed it again.

After a moment, Charlie said, "We're not sure."

Mike turned on him. "But you have an idea. Those kid-things you told me about. You have an idea what they might be?"

"We'll explain in the car," Tim said, motioning for them to get in as he walked around to the driver's side. "Let's go see that house."

Carl Austen was probably never going to bang Carrie Woodward, but he could sure as hell fantasize about it. She was the perfect girl—long black hair, blue eyes, smooth white skin, and the sexiest blow job mouth he'd ever seen. Every time she licked those lips he got hard, and he was pretty sure she knew it. She teased him, flashing him her underwear beneath a short black skirt, rubbing her legs, leaning over so he could see a bit of her bra and occasionally, a peek at a nipple. She had great legs, big breasts, and her ass was so fine…she was smokin' hot, and even if she never let him get past second base, it didn't stop him from picturing every detail about nailing her from every position his limited experience was aware of.

The house was empty that morning, so he didn't have to hide in the bathroom to jerk off. He lay on his back on his bed, flipping through the pictures she'd sent to his phone. She wouldn't agree to send naked pics, but she'd sent some hot ones of her in her underwear, presumably in her bedroom.

He unzipped his pants and grabbed a hold of himself. He

already had an erection just from her pictures. He had just begun to imagine her doing a striptease—he liked his fantasies complete with foreplay, and the striptease was one of his favorites—when there was a loud thump downstairs. He jumped, pulling his hand out of his pants, and sat up, listening. He was annoyed more than anything; he'd been looking forward to some quality alone time, and then video games and maybe a nap. No one else was supposed to be home until five-thirty that evening.

When no further noise came from downstairs, he settled back down onto the bed. His erection had wilted some, but not enough to make it a lost cause. He was about to get back to business when another thump came from downstairs, followed by a giggle. A girl's giggle.

"Dammit." He frowned. Zipping up his pants, he swung his feet over the side of the bed and got up.

"Hello?" he called from the doorway of his room. There was no answer. "Uh, hello?"

"We're down here, Carl," a girl's voice said, followed by more giggling. Two voices, that time.

"The fuck? Who's 'we'?" Carl muttered to himself. He was sure he'd said it too quietly for anyone downstairs to be able to hear, but a response floated up the stairs just the same.

"Come see," the second girl's voice said. She sounded like Carrie. Come to think of it, they both did.

Carl swallowed hard. He was as confused below the belt as above the neck. There shouldn't have been anyone in the house. His mom was "working out" with her yoga teacher and his dad was out, whatever that meant these days when it came to him. They always locked the doors when he was there alone. And... he should have been there alone.

"Come on, Carl," the first girl's voice said. "Come see us. We have a surprise for you."

A flash of unease flushed heat through Carl's face and neck. Something wasn't right here. Yet his feet were carrying him into the hall and toward the stairs. He peered over the railing to the first floor. Whoever was down there wasn't visible from where he was standing. He cleared his throat.

"Who are you?" he called over the railing. There was no

answer. "Hello?" The unease had begun to blossom into actual fear, tugging him away from the railing, away from the first floor. Which was silly, he thought, embarrassed. Assuming the worst, two chicks, probably from school, had broken into his house. He was 6'3". What were they going to do to him, really? Best-case scenario, Carrie had shown up to put her mouth where her promises had been, and she'd brought a friend.

He made himself jog down the steps and then turn the corner to the parlor. Sitting on the couch were two very pale little girls, their gray-tinged skin seeming to waver a little. Carl blinked a few times, but couldn't quite bring the girls into focus, although the couch and everything else around them looked fine. They were cute little girls, with their white little-girl braids and their old-fashioned dresses, and they smiled very sweetly at him. But something was wrong with their eyes. They were entirely black, shining with a kind of malice that Carl felt rather than saw. From the corners of those eyes, that black had begun to marble beneath their skin as if all their hate was leaking into their veins.

The girls stood, making Carl flinch. He flushed with embarrassment and discomfort. They were only little girls.

"Hey, you kids shouldn't be in here," he said, trying to squash the quavering in his voice. "You can't just walk into other people's houses. It's not safe. So get outta here, okay?"

And what if we don't?

They never moved their mouths, but Carl heard the little girl voices as clearly as if they had.

"I'll call your parents, that's what," Carl replied.

Call whoever you like. Call for help.

Scream for help.

We like hearing your kind scream.

The girls' voices bombarded him, excited almost to breathlessness. There was a hysterically gleeful quality to them.

"Look, beat it, okay? You don't belong here. You're gonna be in trouble if I have to—"

Hit us? Is that what you want to do? Do you like to hit little girls?

I think he does. Look at his sex thing in his pants.

He's a bad boy himself.

"No!" Carl shook his head. "No, nothing like that. Jesus." He took a step forward, hoping his size might intimidate them.

"Look, you girls have to—"

He stopped. Their smiles had grown very wide, too impossibly wide, and Carl could see twin caverns of endless teeth. Shards of their skin, broken into irregular patterns by the black marbling of their veins, flaked off and fell to their laps and the couch cushions, and the little glimpses of silvery hate underneath filled Carl with a loathing so intense he could taste it in his mouth. Their fingers, too, had grown long, like hag fingers in some old fairy tale, or gnarled branches of very old trees. The girl on the left used hers to draw long furrows in the arm of the couch.

"Shit," Carl said.

Play with us, Carl. We want you to play with us.

"What the fuck are you?" he whispered, backing away from them slowly, as if retreating from wild dogs. They weren't little girls—that was for sure. They weren't children at all.

Let us show you....

They descended on him before he'd even finished turning to run, and between the two of them, they shredded Carl Austen to easily devoured pieces.

Long before five-thirty in the evening, when Mr. and Mrs. Austen and their youngest son, Andy, returned to a dark, quiet house, all traces of Carl were gone. So were all traces of the two little intruders who had made such quick work of him.

NINE

Slayer's *Seasons in the Abyss* poured out of the speakers in George Clayton's laptop as he took a stolen car for a spin through Vice City. His Xbox One controller vibrated in his hands and he felt a rush of adrenaline as if he were actually behind the wheel. From somewhere in the house below, his ma yelled at him to turn the music down—at least, that's what he thought she was screaming, but it was hard to hear her over the music. She didn't care much for what he liked to listen to, and often didn't seem to care much for him, but he'd learned to live with that. She was a tough old bitch to make happy, and some days, he didn't have it in him to try.

He felt the buzz of his cell rather than heard it and paused both the game and the music to check who was calling.

"Finally! Thank you!" his mother's shrill voice carried up the stairs, sounding anything but grateful.

Scowling at his closed bedroom door as if the woman far beyond it could see him, he scooped up his cell and saw Mike was calling. He pushed the Accept button and said, "Hey, man?"

"Hey. What're you doing?" Mike sounded very far away, almost as if his voice was echoing down a long tunnel.

"Playing GTA. What're you up to?"

From the other end of the line, muted sounds indicated Mike was lighting a cigarette. He exhaled an odd distortion of air into the phone. "I'm at the house."

"Your house?"

"No," the echo of Mike said, puffing on the cigarette. "The house. You know. From the other night."

George shrugged off the twinge of discomfort he felt at the

mention of *that* house. He wasn't sure what had happened, if anything, but since that night, he'd been having headaches. He'd also been losing little snatches of time—twenty minutes here, thirty minutes there. Sometimes the clock indicated it was much later than it should have been. Sometimes, it was much earlier. And he'd been hearing things. His mom said they were random house sounds, but they sounded close, behind, or around him, and he'd never noticed them before.

"Why?" George shifted on the bed.

"Come meet us here," Mike replied.

"Like fuck I will," George said. "I ain't going back there, man."

"Don't be a pussy. You're in trouble and we can help."

George frowned into the phone. "What do you mean?"

"Someone knows what we did in that house."

"So what? We didn't do anything. I mean, not really." George fidgeted with a loose thread on his bedspread. They'd been drinking and smoking pot. It was dark. There were parts he couldn't entirely remember. But he was pretty sure the vague disquiet he had been feeling since that night had more to do with the dreams he had been having of the place and not of the place itself.

"Yeah, we did. You know that. And someone killed Pete and Carl over it. You want to be next?" Mike's voice had taken on a sinister quality which surprised George as much as unsettled him.

"What? You're kidding."

"No, I'm not. Shit's real, and it's bad."

George thought he heard a faint giggle on the other end of the line, and something like a growl. Mike was messing with him.

He had to be.

"Dude, how fucking stupid do you think I am? Come on, stop fucking with me."

"See for yourself if I am."

A moment later, the phone in his hand beeped and he flinched. He pulled the phone away from his ear and saw a notification for a new text message.

"Go ahead," the tinny voice on the line told him. "Check it."

George clicked on the text message and a picture popped up.

At first, all George could make out was a mess of red. His brain couldn't quite wrap around the details—the fingers in the bottom left corner, the bit of sneaker, the clump of matted hair. Carl's wallet on a chain.

Carl's wallet. Oh my God.

Then the mass of red coalesced into bodies, two of them, lying mangled on a blood-splattered wooden floor. The one George thought was Carl lay face down, a pool of blood spreading out from what was left of his slightly turned head. His right leg was bent the wrong way at the knee, creating a triangle shape that cast the whole scene as somewhat surreal. Those mangled things couldn't have been the bodies of his friends, not bent like that...could they? The wallet seemed to say so. Pete's hair, strawberry-tinted by the wounds on his head, seemed to say so.

George's stomach lurched. "What the fuck?" he whispered. It didn't occur to him until a few seconds after that Mike had no business having those pictures on the phone in the first place. George was about say so when his friend spoke again.

"So much blood, huh?" The voice sounded further down that tunnel and less like anyone George had ever met. He didn't like it.

"Mike—"

"Never mind the house, Georgie. We've come to you. We're already here," the voice said, sliding from Mike's register into that of a child and then down into something so low and malevolent that George tore the phone away from his head.

From somewhere deep inside the cell came the giggling. It was awful, that hysterical mirth. He jabbed the button to end the call and tossed the cell away from him. It clattered on the floor and slid a foot or so toward the far side of the room, and yet George thought he still heard the giggling. He fought the urge to follow it and stomp on the laughter. He didn't want to go near it again.

Instead, George grabbed his keys and bolted from the room,

taking the stairs so fast that he nearly twisted his ankle when his foot skidded over the edge of a step.

"George?" his mom called from the living room as he jumped the remaining stairs to the first floor.

"Going out," he managed to say. He wasn't sure if she'd heard him or not and didn't care. He was already out the front door.

In the sunlight, what had happened in his bedroom didn't seem real. Had it been an acid flashback? Had Jeremy laced one of his cigarettes again for laughs? Motherfucker. George shook his head and then pinched the bridge of his nose. A slight headache was forming just behind his eyes. He looked around. No one was there. Certainly, no one like the voice on the phone was anywhere in sight. He moved cautiously down the front steps and turned toward the driveway, heading for his car. His keys dangled from shaking fingers.

As he got into the car, he reached in his pocket for his cell, remembered he'd tossed it upstairs, and swore to himself. He wanted to call Mike and find out what the hell was going on. It seemed imperative to him that he talk to his friend, if for no other reason than to make sure Mike, the real Mike, was still there to talk to, still *himself*. He needed that tether to reality after...after whatever the hell had happened upstairs.

He pulled out of the driveway and onto the street, glancing a few times at the house, particularly the upstairs window where his bedroom was. The irrational part of him that had fanned the embers of panic into full-blown flames expected the voice in the phone to somehow crawl out of it, materializing into something that was not Mike, something that would come crashing out of the window and chase after his car. He swallowed, forcing his gaze back on the road.

He was almost out of his development when he happened to glance in the rearview and see two children in the back seat, prim and pale and silent. He jumped and the car swerved. Immediately he pulled over to the curb, threw the car in Park and whirled around.

He'd seen enough horror movies to genuinely believe that checking the back seat, he'd find the children had disappeared.

They hadn't, though; a little boy and a little girl in colorless, old-fashioned clothing sat holding hands, watching him intently. They were so pale-skinned, a white that was almost gray, and so still that a horrifying if irrational thought overwhelmed him. What if they were dead? What if the owner of the voice on the phone had somehow put dead children in his car to frame him, or maybe they had gotten in to play a game and, unable to get out again, had suffocated in his back seat? What would he do? How would he explain it to anyone?

George was afraid to touch them. He swallowed a few times to force down the gorge rising in his throat. He'd always had a nervous stomach, and it was doing cartwheels just then. Dead children? What had—

Then the boy tilted his head and George screamed.

"Who are you?" he yelled at them. "You scared me half to death, you know? What the hell you doin' in my car?"

The little girl giggled. She had a crack running zigzags from her right eyebrow nearly to her pale-blonde hairline. It reminded George of the kind of crack one might see on an old doll.

"We came for you, silly," she said.

The boy's placid expression didn't change, but he nodded.

"For me?" George couldn't pin down any of the thoughts whizzing around his head, other than that something about all this was very wrong.

"For you," the girl said.

George thought about telling them to get out, just get the hell out of his car. He didn't; they were little kids without a parent and they looked sick, and years of his ma's yelling about manners and being a man stood resolutely in the way of gut instinct. Instead, he said, "Look, I don't have time to play. How about I just drive you home, huh?"

"You can't get there from here," the boy said with disinterest.

"Not in that body," the girl added, and giggled again.

That time, George recognized the giggle. It was the one from the phone.

His eyes grew wide. "You," he breathed, and scrambled for the door handle. A grip like steel clamped down on his arm and wrenched it free of the door. He heard something inside his wrist crack. Another grabbed his other arm and he was hoisted out of the driver's seat and yanked toward the back. George screamed again. The children's hands were free, and it took George a moment or two to realize that what held him so tightly were tentacles coming from the children's stomachs.

"Fuck, let me go!" George screamed, his own arms flailing, his fists pounding at anything he could reach. "No! No!!"

He saw the girl's mouth widen into a smile, her chin dropping as her jaw unhinged. His fist connected with one of her eyes and he felt something hot and gelatinous seep through his fingers and begin to burn as it travelled across the back of his hand. He heard the bones in his arm crack before he actually felt any pain, but when the latter came, it too was hot and horrible.

George managed to scream once more before the children in his back seat devoured him alive.

TEN

"So let me get this straight," Mike said. "You're telling me that we summoned some kind of demons that look like missing children going back what, twenty years?"

"That's what we believe, yes," Tim said from the front seat. He was driving, and Mike, when he wasn't distracted, was giving directions from the back. Tim exchanged glances with Charlie in the passenger seat. "We're not sure if they're using the children's actual bodies or just mimicking them, but they aren't children at all. They're savage and dangerous."

"And these things are coming after us? Why?"

"Who knows? Maybe when you guys did that ritual, you blew something up in their world and they're pissed. Maybe something Scott said in that other language was a direct invitation to attack us all. Or hell, maybe they're just mean sons of bitches and they like killing."

"So what do we do?"

"Well first," Tim said, "we check out the house. Let's see what went on there, if anything was left behind that we can use to reverse what they did. Then we go get the others, hopefully before the children do. Try George and Carl again."

Mike dialed George, then Carl, but shook his head. "Nothing. They're not answering."

"Damn it," Tim muttered. "Who lives closest to that old house?"

"Well," Mike said hesitantly, "actually, that would be Jeremy and Scott."

Jeremy and Scott Clinton sat in the back yard drinking beers. Their stepbrothers and sisters, little monsters all, were out, probably breaking things all around the neighborhood. Their father was at his second job at the mill and their mother didn't much care what they did so long as the cops didn't show up at the door and nothing caught on fire. She was a woman who managed to look soused and dried up at the same time, with messily-bound hair the color and texture of bleached straw and both a face and a fist that made drinking outside, despite her indifference to most things, preferrable than next to her on the couch as she sat smoking Parliaments and bitching that her checks were late.

Jeremy flipped through the book he'd gotten at that old man's garage sale. He'd lifted it, naturally; paying for things was for the slow and the weak. Jeremy was neither, in his mind. The old man hadn't noticed. He had to have been half-blind not to have noticed such a gigantic doorstop gone missing. It wasn't like Jeremy had put the bulky thing under his T-shirt; he'd simply picked it up and walked away with it. It was only when Jeremy was a block or two away with his new prize that it briefly occurred to him that maybe the old man had wanted to be rid of the book anyway. Maybe, just maybe, it wasn't Jeremy who had pulled a fast one.

That was, of course, silly. The book was priceless in certain circles. Jeremy knew just enough about occult shit from his brother and his own reading to know *The Book of Doors* when he saw it, and to recognize its value. It was an English translation, probably with all the good stuff cut out, but it was damn well worth more than being relegated to some cheap folding table in a driveway summer garage sale. He could sell it...or keep it, maybe.

The book itself was worn around the edges and on the faded maroon fabric covers. Raised silver lettering proclaimed its title in a language neither of the boys recognized, but Jeremy had seen pictures on certain obscure internet sites, and he knew what he held in his hands. Most of that occult stuff was bullshit—for the same slow, weak sheep that thought shoplifting or smoking a joint was walking on the wild side. The world was made to suck and if people could fix it by mumbling a few old words and waving jazz hands, then they would. Fact was, it didn't work.

Still, he'd heard stories...rumors that *The Book of Doors* was a different sort of thing. He'd found the spell they'd tried at the old house in the book, and had to admit that when nothing materialized, he'd been disappointed.

Then he'd started having the dreams, the ones in which dead children peeled off the skin of his face a strip at a time and made him read what was written underneath, the story of his soul. They did other unbearably painful things, too—things his brain immediately purged upon waking, but whose horrors lingered just below the surface of conscious thought.

And it wasn't just the dreams—there were the weird flickers out of the corner of his eye, the little sharp movements and muffled sounds. He'd find himself standing in the kitchen sometimes and although it only felt like a few minutes, an hour had gone by. He'd thought he'd heard a child's giggling from the azalea bush on the side of the house the other day, and last night, he'd seen it—one of the dead children from his dream. She might have been cute once before the decay had begun hollowing out her blackened eye sockets and the corners of her mouth. Her white hair hung in limp pigtails, and her old-fashioned clothes, where torn, showed the bruised little body was giving way to bone.

No, not bone...whatever whitish, silverish thing she really was underneath.

Very little scared Jeremy, but he was instantly terrified of the girl.

He'd shouted to her, even took a step toward her, but the way she smiled, too wide and too sharp-toothed, made him bolt back into the house. A check from the windows showed she had gone, but Jeremy shook all over.

Maybe something *had* actually happened in the old house.

He hadn't told Scott, of course. His brother was too big and too dumb to appreciate the implications. He sat in the lawn chair next to Jeremy crushing empty beer cans and occasionally bitching about how reading was for assholes, while Jeremy flipped through the book. If he'd been able to find something on one of those pages to let that little monster through a door, then maybe he could find something to send it back.

He had to send it back.

The shimmering edges of the rip between universes yawned wide. Mr. Triangle waited impatiently for Miss Circle and the others. The Fractal growled and keened and rotated beyond. Mr. Triangle couldn't see it through the rip, but he could feel it. It had waited eons for a physical world to conquer, and now that the shapes were so close to cementing their hold on this world, the great being was growing impatient. Mr. Triangle certainly couldn't hold it back, nor did he think he could convince it not to begin devolving and re-evolving the new world in endless spirals of destruction and new creation, even if doing so before the kills were completed might cause destabilization of...well, everything. Miss Circle could usually placate its impatience, but only a little and only for a short while. Mr. Triangle wished she would hurry back. There were six kills left, and Mr. Triangle knew the others were already feeling the aches and pulls on the physical frames they had stolen. Timeliness was important. Even Mr. Hexagon couldn't argue that point, though he argued everything else.

Mr. Triangle approximated a sigh. He'd seen one of the creatures do it and it had amused him. He'd found the sigh was a pleasant release of his frustration. Plus, it impressed the others that he had mastered a physical act.

A moment later, he felt the tight little vibrations in the air that meant another was coming. He was about to give Miss Circle a sigh of disapproval when he was startled to see a tiny portion of The Fractal emerging through the rip. Had Mr. Triangle mastered the gasp, he might have done so then.

That was it, then. The Fractal was coming.

The parts of The Book of Doors about closing said doors were far more difficult than the ones about opening them. It was generally considered almost impossible to open a door, and absolutely impossible to do it by accident, so if all the conditions lined up and a door actually opened, very little could be done to stop or reverse that. Jeremy found some promising lines in "Chapter 18—Limiting Ingress and Egress", but as he began to read them out loud, he frowned. An asterisk led to a footnote which indicated the spell was incomplete. He had thought "unabridged" might mean he could undo whatever bridge or door he'd opened, but that was apparently not the case.

"Fuck it," he said to Scott, who was dozing on the chair, a beer can still clutched in one meaty hand. "I'm gonna try it anyway."

"No," a little voice from behind him said.

It was the dead girl.

"What the fuck are you?" Jeremy whispered, rising from his seat.

"Let me show you," she said, and with her little fingers, she split open her ribcage and showed him the universe inside.

His head felt heavy and his vision blurred. He might have dropped the book; he was vaguely aware that he no longer felt its weight in his hands, and something...something was on fire at his feet. A faraway part of his brain told him to grab it, to save those pages about closing the doors, but when he reached in the direction of the book, or at least what he thought was the direction, a splitting pain on the side of his head made him wince. His fingers felt squeezed and then crushed. If they made a sound, it was lost to the roaring in his head, like the screaming...someone was screaming his name....

He saw nothing else but that swirling of galaxies and stars and planets contained inside the little girl. And then the stars parted and the galaxies spun away, and there was nothing but the frigid black of starless space, beyond the edge of the universe and before the edges of any other one. Jeremy felt sick and elated at the same time, and whatever might have been holding him together as a civilized member of the human race finally snapped. The black from inside the little girl came out and swallowed his own insides, and he fell to the ground.

ELEVEN

When they approached the old house, it was already getting dark. Orange and purple streaked across the sky, and shadows grew longer, wrapping around the car and sinking into the cracks of the street. It felt colder, too, much colder than it should have for June, and as they came to a stop at the curb in front of the old house, there was a notable difference in the air. It was as if a late-autumn night had suddenly rushed in, drawing out the life and warmth of the day, muting its colors and stealing its breath. A low wail carried to the car, though whether it was from the wind or from something stirring in the remains of the old house, Tim couldn't tell.

The boys glanced at each other. If they noticed a glitch in the day/night cycle or the weather, they opted to keep it to themselves.

"This the place?" Tim asked.

Mike nodded. "Yeah, that's the place."

Tim opened the car door. "Well, let's get to it."

Charlie followed suit. Mike muttered something under his breath and shook his head.

"What?" Charlie hung in the car doorway.

"I said I think I'll wait here," Mike said. "Once in that house was enough for me."

"I don't think any of us should be alone," Tim said through the window.

Mike gave him an exaggerated sigh and got out of the car. As the three of them made their way over the grass, Tim noticed an odd crunching beneath their feet. The closer they got, the stiffer the grass became, until it gave way to hard-packed dirt beneath their feet. Behind him, one of the boys kicked something that clinked like a beer bottle and Tim flinched in spite of himself.

The old house was only still a house by the loosest definition. The colonial stone foundations were there, and most of the four walls remained standing, but there was nearly nothing left of the roof. It only stood one floor, and contained three, maybe four small rooms, based on the size of it. Long two-by-fours had been nailed haphazardly across the door, and all the windows were boarded up except for the right front window. It glared at them like a single malevolent eye. Stagnant shadows clung like a film to the place, and Tim could almost swear the musty rot smell was coming from those irregular patches of darkness.

"That how you got in?" Charlie asked, gesturing at the window.

"Yeah." Mike crossed his arms over his chest and looked away.

Tim tapped the flashlight app on his phone and approached the window, shining the light through. The partitions between rooms had rotted through, leaving just the frames. The majority of the house was now one large open room. The floor was littered with dead leaves, dark clumps that could have been the beginnings of mulch or rotting and forgotten rags, and broken beams of splintered wood.

A twang of pain stabbed into his brain, and Tim saw again the walls of a bloody house in space. It had been this house he'd seen in one of his visions. He blinked several times and shook his head.

"You okay?" he heard Charlie ask behind him.

"Yeah. Yeah," Tim said. "I'm fine." He swept the phone light across the floor again and saw the waxen lumps that had been candles. There were nine of them, evenly spaced in a ring between two concentric chalk circles on the floor. The chalk was badly smudged, probably from the scuffling feet of the boys who had drunk themselves into languorous stupors after what they thought had been a failed attempt at a dark ritual.

He withdrew the flashlight and was about to turn away when a glint of light caught his eye.

"What is it?" Mike asked. The boys had come up alongside

him and were watching his face anxiously.

"I don't know," Tim muttered, and shined the light in the direction of the glint. At first, he saw nothing. The room was empty, and he could see nothing metallic or reflective in any way.

Then an arc of the light caught the air in the center of the room at just such an angle that he saw it again—a flash of brightness that struck him as unnatural. His first thought was that it was oily somehow, that sliver of brightness. Colors swirled where they shouldn't have been visible.

"Did you guys see that?" he asked.

"See what?" Mike asked.

Tim moved the light back and forth until it caught the sliver of swirling light again, and the boys gasped.

"Was that there when you guys did the ritual?" Charlie asked.

"No," Mike said. "There wasn't anything there like that. I swear."

"I'm going in," Tim said. He tucked the phone into his shirt pocket so that the light shined outward, then planted a hand on each side of the windowsill. It wasn't set very high up on the wall, and Tim thought he could get a leg up, but it was a narrow fit. After some grunting and pushing, he managed to shove himself through the window and landed with a puff of stale dust on the floor. It creaked in weak protest of his weight.

"Want us to come in, too?" Charlie and Mike crowded the window from the other side.

"No, you guys stay there for the moment," Tim said, holding up a hand. Let me see what this thing is first." He crept closer to the place where he'd seen the oily brightness, and as he got closer to the center of the room, he became aware by degrees of a different smell, one he couldn't place. It was an acrid, smoky smell, like something chemical that had been burning. It hurt his nose and the back of his throat, and he tucked the lower half of his face beneath the neck of his shirt to try to filter it out.

He took the phone-light out of his pocket and moved it around, trying to catch the sliver of light again. When he saw it, his breath caught. It looked to him like a vertical, free-floating oval of oil-spill, a nauseous churning of clear fluid tinged gray and veined with swirling colors. It was framed with something that had the shape and texture of ragged tears of skin, but was pale, like the skin of the dead. The edges moved in and out as if something from beyond was inhaling and exhaling its breath between worlds. That burning smell was strongest just at the mouth of the strangeness...the *doorway.*

It was some kind of doorway.

He could feel it, the certainty of it pulsing with the throb in his head. The children-things had come through here. The shapes.

"I found it," Tim said.

"What is it?" Charlie asked from beyond the window. Just then, he seemed a hundred miles away, down a long tunnel.

"I think it's how they came here, those things. The children. I think it's their door."

"Whose door?" a voice behind him said.

Tim wheeled around, his heart pounding.

Jeremy stepped from a swath of shadows. A long, bloody scratch from temple to jawline had split his face, and blood had spilled down his neck and into the collar of his shirt. He was nursing his left hand in his right, and though it was hard to tell in the dimness, the fingers of the left looked twisted into knots and kinks that fingers shouldn't make. The perpetual smirk that Jeremy wore like armor had fallen away, and what stood before Tim was scared and broken, and not the cynical and sinister boy Tim had come to distrust.

"Jeremy? What the fuck, man?" Mike said from the window. "Where did you come from?"

"What happened?" Tim asked more softly. "Who did that to you?"

"You called them children. They're not. They're not children," Jeremy said, shaking his head.

"I know," Tim replied. He considered reaching out a reassuring hand to clap Jeremy on the shoulder and decided against it.

"They killed Scott," Jeremy said. His voice was flat, as if the words still didn't feel real. He seemed to go away somewhere in his head for a moment—maybe back to whatever had happened to his brother—and then suddenly looked at Tim. "There are so many of them. And they're only paving the way."

"Paving the way? For what? What do you mean?"

A long, low wail erupted from beyond the swirling film, and they all turned back to the portal.

"From that," Jeremy whispered. Then he began to laugh.

TWELVE

Tim was vaguely aware in the periphery of his sight that Jeremy had fled into the darkness outside the little shell of house, although he hadn't climbed through the same window Tim had used. One moment he was there in the house with Tim, and the next, Tim could hear the boy's laughing, lunatic whooping more akin to war cries than mirth, floating back on the still, stale summer air.

Tim meant to follow but couldn't. He couldn't have turned away from the shimmering swirl of colors even if he'd tried. They had taken on a sickish kind of hue, not quite green or gray or yellow but some ugly shade among them. Now, they filled the space of his vision, the scope of his conscious attention, and although somewhere deep down, his brain was screaming a warning to look away, it was like a voice in a dream, soundless and soft and blurred beneath more pressing thoughts.

"Jenks? Mr. Jenkins, what is that? Get out of there, man. I really think you should—"

Tim could hear Charlie at the window, but the rest of what he was saying got lost in the music from the nauseating colors. They were making a kind of tinkling melody with their movements, like the gears of some ancient music box. It might have been pretty, except in conjunction with the colors, they felt more like little slivers of glass, poking and prodding the nauseated places in him. From some place beyond the music and the mumble of Charlie's voice, Mike shouted at Jeremy to come back, but if Jeremy answered, the words were lost to Tim.

"Mr. Jenkins!" Charlie's voice was closer now, but it didn't matter. The swirling colors had formed an oval long enough for a man to step through, and now that shimmering space was widening. He thought he saw movement beyond the colors, oily and indefinite shapes that skittered and stopped, lurched and jerked.

Jeremy was right. Something was coming.

"Jenks!" A hand roughly grabbed his arm and began pulling him away. At first he didn't want to go, but once his feet got moving, the music faded and the colors bled away. Then he and Charlie and Mike were running in the dark, scrambling over the uneven ground back to the car, tumbling inside, driving away.

It was several minutes before the outside world found its way back to Tim's senses. His voice followed shortly after, and as he realized Charlie was driving, he frowned.

"How'd you get the keys?" he asked Charlie.

The boy glanced at him. "You gave them to me before I put you in the car, remember?"

Tim didn't, but he offered a weak smile and nodded anyway.

"So, what the fuck was that back there?" Mike asked. "Now that you're, like, you again, Mr. Jenks...what happened?"

Tim shook his head slowly. "I—I don't know. It was...some kind of hole. A portal, maybe. I don't know. I just remember the colors and the music."

"What music?" Charlie asked.

"What happened to Jeremy?" Tim asked, ignoring Charlie's question.

"He ran," Mike answered, and waved good riddance to the memory. "Bastard was laughing like a psycho. I ran after—followed him to the street, but he ducked behind a car and by the time I got there...I dunno. He bolted, I guess. He was gone. Couldn't see him anywhere."

He leaned forward. "Anyway, who cares? What happened to you in the house, man?"

Tim closed his eyes. His head ached, and behind his eyelids he could see flashes of vision intermingled with the shapeless movement from beyond the swirling colors. In one of the snippets of vision, the dead children surrounded a house, a different one this time, and they were humming. In another, Charlie and

Mike were quivering lumps of diced-up flesh spread out over a hardwood floor. One flash showed his abdomen cut open, and black fluids were pouring out in torrents all over his shoes.

He squinted and shook his head. "The thing on the other side was coming through. I don't know what it is or what it has to do with those child-things, but I think it's bad. Bad news, worse than anything we've seen yet. I don't understand it all, but I think that thing is what the children, the shapes, are getting ready for. I think it's the thing the ritual really unleashed. We need to go back. We need to stop it, whatever it is. We need to—"

"Are you nuts?" Charlie's voice was low, that serious, no-nonsense man-voice that he'd picked up in the last few days that worried Tim. "We can't go back there."

"We have to!" Tim said. "Or I have to, rather. I should drop you boys off. Right. Stay together tonight—stay put until I come for you. And if I don't—"

"Did he hit his head in there?" Mike asked Charlie.

"You can't go back there," Charlie said. "If something's coming through, we need to know how to fight it. And we don't. Didn't you always tell us we had to do our research? To think before acting and all that?"

The boy had a point. Tim sat back in the seat, groaning. "Okay, yeah. You're right. We need to find Jeremy and figure out what, exactly, we need to do to close this door. And we've got to gather supplies—occult paraphernalia we might need. Not novelty stuff, but the real thing."

"And where do we get that?"

"I think I might know a guy," Mike said from the back seat.

Charlie let out a long, low breath. "Okay then. Let's do it."

THIRTEEN

The shimmering light in the abandoned ruins of the old house pulsated and pulled, yawning and stretching. Had there been anyone left there to observe it, he or she might have seen vague forms moving just beyond the swirls of colors, silhouettes of inhuman geometry and proportion. One might have heard a sound like heavy gears turning, if such gears were old and just awakening to movement. In the world beyond the swirling colors, the world Mr. Triangle and the other shapes were so intent on escaping, things moved with mind-numbing slowness most times, and then skipped like old records, and suddenly things were happening. Speech, such as it ever was, drew sound and syllables out in odd ways, making them stretch and yawn like the light until they nearly broke, and any meaning they might have been holding tumbled away. There was no sense in having stable bodies anymore, not there. And it was foolish to call any part of it home, because it was falling apart. Like the world of the Hollowers so many aeons ago, the world beyond the swirls was unstable, its laws of physics irregular and dangerous.

It was time to go.

The shapes knew that. They hadn't wanted to admit it aloud, not to each other or even to themselves, but they knew how important solidifying their hold in this new dimension would be. Timeliness and completing the kills, and in the right order, was crucial.

And the shapes weren't the only ones who knew this, although the Fractal had undoubtedly been slower in its realization.

The Fractal wouldn't need to possess the forms of dead

children. Like the Hollowers, it wouldn't need a physical body to own this new world. Its presence alone would begin to change things, to turn physicality inside out. Everything it touched would be affected by the change, and soon, this new world would be like their old one. For a time, that would be just fine, so long as the shapes gathered the blood and bones they needed. It wouldn't be permanent stability—nothing was ever permanent, not in this dimension or any other—but it would do for a good, long time.

Then someday, when the instability of conflicting physics overtook it, the new world would be abandoned just as others in the past were, and they would move on. The shapes just hoped there were other dimensions with beings as reckless as this one, summoners capable of understanding the rites and rituals to open doors.

This world had *Le Livre des Portes*. This world had dead children.

Maybe the next would have similar things...or maybe not.

When the shapes returned to the house, they could feel that something was different—not so different as to mean the Fractal had crossed over; if anything, it had receded, strangely enough, perhaps gathering its strength to push through the barrier. Rather, Mr. Triangle sensed echoes of the beings of this world. They left a trace of themselves, a faint glow where they touched things. Many dimensions' living creatures, whether physical or not, did this. Mr. Triangle suspected that most of the beings didn't know what they left behind, and that was okay. The shapes could sense the residue and that was enough. Little tricks of the predator, Mr. Decagon used to say. The tracking signs were there if one knew how to look.

The glow indicated the beings had come to the shapes rather than the other way around, and Mr. Triangle was both amused and annoyed. On the one hand, the beings had seen the rip, and likely, the Fractal beyond. Mr. Triangle could smell the fear and confusion in their glow. Of course, an opportunity had been missed; a summoner and the two keys had come to *their* spot, *their* rip, while the shapes were busy with others.

Miss Circle joined him at the mouth of the rip. Her little hand took his and held it. It was something they had discovered the beings of this world did, and although they hadn't completely pieced together why, it was a pleasant thing, a thing that stimulated feeling in these new bodies. The two stood silently, holding each other's hand and staring into the rip, for several long minutes.

After a while, she thought to him. *It's coming, isn't it?*

Yes. Soon.

That must mean it's getting worse over there.

It doesn't matter anymore. We're here now.

What if we can't stay?

Mr. Triangle looked at her. *Why wouldn't we be able to stay?*

Miss Circle returned his gaze. *I don't know. I don't claim to understand these bodies...but some of the others are talking.*

They're wrong. Mr. Triangle looked away. In truth, he didn't know if they were or not, but he had to believe they were. He had thought the bodies of the dead children were stable, and on that premise, he'd brought them all through the rip. The bodies had taken some work to unearth and reconstruct—some of them had been missing, buried, or even under water a very long time—but they seemed solid. There wouldn't be another incident like before, with Mr. Decagon. He believed that...most of the time.

So many over there will be lost, Miss Circle thought at him.

They are not our problem.

No, she silently agreed, *they are not. Then, when?*

Soon.

She squeezed his hand gently, another thing she'd learned from watching this world's beings. *And those things—the rituals with those things—will let us stay? Keep us from falling apart?*

Yes. We need fear in the blood. Stress in the bones. When we have those things, all will be right.

Are you scared? she asked him.

No.

Then neither am I. She let go of his hand and turned to join the others. A few feet away, she paused and turned back to him.

Let's kill the rest of them soon.

He nodded. She smiled at him and skipped off.

Mr. Triangle listened to the others chatting silently in thoughts but kept his own hidden. He brooded in front of the rip for a long, long time.

They were taking to this new world; they had to be. He knew it because Miss Circle hadn't known he was lying to her.

FOURTEEN

Mike directed them to a little dead-end street on the far side of town. The neighborhood was one of those places forgotten by the development of the rest of the area. The houses were old and beginning to show it, the lawns overgrown, the windows more often than not boarded up. Tim noticed there were no mailboxes, either affixed to the houses or posted at the curb, and no house numbers that he could see, and he wondered how it was even possible for someone to live on that street.

"There, that's it," Mike said, pointing at a once-white house three up from the end of the street. It was a bi-level with black shutters and careless shrubbery overtaking either side of the front steps. Its siding made Tim think of a white garbage bag stretched tight over sharp things, though he couldn't quite pinpoint any particular feature of the place that conjured the image.

"Here? You're sure someone lives here?" he asked with a raised eyebrow.

"I'm sure. I've bought weed off this guy like, a hundred times."

Tim turned around in the passenger seat. "You brought us to your drug dealer? Seriously?"

Mike looked nettled. "That's not all he does," he said. "You'll see."

They got out of the car and followed Mike to the door. The boy knocked twice before they heard shuffling from the other side and the door cracked open. The skinny old man on the other side, wrapped in a pale blue, threadbare bathrobe over black sweatpants, looked as if Tim and the others had interrupted his hangover. Despite the beginnings of a receding hairline, most of his hair was long and pulled back into a messy ponytail. The scruff on his chin indicated he hadn't shaved in days. The bags under his eyes suggested he hadn't really slept in at least that long.

He blinked a few times at Tim and Charlie, then turned to the only familiar face on his doorstep.

"Mike? I told you, buddy, I'm, uh, 'light' 'til next week."

Mike shook his head. "I'm not here for weed, dude. We need to talk to you."

The guy gave Tim a suspicious look. "Oh yeah? About what?"

"Some fucked-up otherworld shit. You were right. Little monsters like kids and a hole in, like, reality in an old, abandoned farmhouse. And possibly the end of the world."

The man considered this for a second, yawned, and said, "Don't know what the hell took you so long," then ushered them inside.

The living room of the house looked pretty much like Tim figured it would. There were empty beer cans littering the top and surrounding the legs of a small battered coffee table, as well as empty, half-crushed packs of cigarettes. A ratty sofa faded into the background gloom of the place, while a reclining easy chair, dotted with cigarette burns, faced a tiny television.

The man led them through that room into an unused dining room whose central table was piled high with stacks of papers and laundry, to a door at the back of a small, stained kitchen. The door opened onto a flight of badly painted stairs and the miasma of mildew. Tim and the boys followed the man down into the depths of an unfinished basement which, to Tim's amazement, had been converted into a room for monitoring the cosmos...or whatever lay beyond it.

A large wooden table stood in the center of the concrete floor between two gray pillars. Spread out on its surface were a series of star and constellation maps sprinkled with Post-it notes on which the man had jotted down notes. Behind the table on a painter's easel was a large corkboard like what Tim imagined detective offices used to follow details of a case. This particular board had charts and graphs pinned to it, as well as black and white and color photos of various government-looking people in business attire. Some of the items were marked "CERN" in green, others marked "MK OSSIUM" in red, and yet others marked "ANTARCTICA PROJECT" in blue. There was also a map of the United States with pushpins, and scribbled notes indicating which were portals, triangles, "soft spots," gateways, and interdimensional doorways.

"What is this place?" Charlie asked in amazement. He picked up an oddly shaped black glass object which the man immediately took from his hand and replaced with great care on the table.

"This," Mike said, partly in amusement and partly with pride, "is Hank Denver's war room."

"That's me," the man said, scratching at his arm. "I'm Hank. That's me."

"Never much believed in any of it, but there you go," Mike added.

After Tim and Charlie introduced themselves, Hank asked them a series of "security" questions, as he put it, and then scanned them with some cheap, plastic-looking handheld thing. He examined the results, and seemingly satisfied, put the instrument back on the table.

"Sorry," he said. "Can't be too careful." What he had to be careful about, Tim didn't know, but he figured if it put the man's mind at ease to scan them with his toy, so be it. Still, it was a waste of time on their part, and on the part of this crackpot dope dealer. For all his charts and graphs, the man was obviously a few pins short of a bowling lane, and Tim couldn't see how anything he had to say would be of much assistance.

"Hank, we need your help," Mike said.

"Mike, maybe we've bothered Mr. Denver enough for one day," Tim cut in, gesturing that they should leave.

"No, no, it's okay," Denver said. "It's no trouble at all. Mike here was right to bring you. I'll tell you, it's a small world. I had no idea you were targets. It's good you came to me first."

"Oh?" Tim said.

"Yeah. I've been watching this sort of thing for decades. It doesn't happen often, but hoo-boy, when it does, it makes quite a fuck of a mess."

"You can say that again," Charlie said.

"What sort of thing?" Tim asked.

Denver looked at him as if he were being dense. "The opening of doorways, man. Interdimensional portals. The invasion of intraterrestrial entities, particularly the type bent on significantly altering or destroying, in whole or in part, the universe as we know it."

"Well," Tim replied, doing his best to keep his skepticism in check as he peered down at the papers on the table, "what we're up against is more than something on charts and graphs and old declassified documents. We're in serious trouble, Mr. Denver, and while I'm sure you mean well with all of this, we have a real, serious situation and I really don't think—"

"I know better than you what you're up against, Mr. Tim," Denver said. "This ain't my first rodeo, dig?"

"Okay, surprise me then. Tell me what you know."

"I'll take a stab at it and say they look like dead children," Denver said, and his tone sent a chill up Tim's spine. "They aren't children, of course, but the bodies are easy to find and manipulate, and they have about as much self-control. Oh, they're little monsters alright, as Mike called them. And if you're talking about them coming through the hole in the farmhouse out by the cemetery, then they're only going to be the beginning, if we don't get a move on."

"You've seen them?" Tim asked, astounded.

"I've been watching them, same as any other interdimensional invader. Mike and his dumbass friends let them in. No offense," he said to Charlie.

"None taken," Charlie responded.

"Anyway, the point is, if you want to stop the shapes," Denver said, "then I know how."

FIFTEEN

Hank Denver went to a computer in the corner of the room and sat in the rolling chair. He began to type at the keyboard and the screen in front of him sprang to life. Line after line of complex mathematical formulas beyond Tim's grasp began to scroll across the computer monitor, and Denver made satisfied grunts and nods. When he stopped typing, the formulas ran for a few more lines, blinked, then cleared, offering a single formula in response.

Denver scratched his scruffy chin. "This is bad," he said.

"What is? What's bad?" Tim asked over the man's shoulder.

Denver rolled around to face him. "Your farmhouse portal," he replied. "It's open, in spite of the supremely sloppy and idiotic fumblings of Mike's friends—many of whom, I'm assuming, have been devoured or mangled in some way already."

Charlie and Mike looked from Denver to Tim and back to Denver but didn't speak. Tim forgot sometimes that despite all their independence, they were still just children. Their being alone in the world was a sad thing, but not nearly so sad as when situations made it all the more obvious that Tim was the only real source of authority or security those kids had.

"Mr. Denver, please," Tim said. "If the portal is open, just tell us how to close it before anyone else gets hurt. Tell us how to send those things away."

"The shapes," Denver said thoughtfully.

"Yes, the shapes."

"Well, we can try reversing the ritual," Denver said.

"Dude, you don't sound very confident," Mike said.

"This isn't a science," Denver replied, unruffled, "despite all those formulas and whatnot. There's an element of finesse, of gut instinct. Of...guesswork."

"We're screwed," Charlie mumbled, throwing up his hands. "We're all going to die."

Denver grinned, a wild, incongruent twist of the face. "Not necessarily, boy. We have one advantage."

"Oh? And what's that?" Tim asked, glancing from the formula to the old man's face.

"Stability. Material stability in a home dimension meant for us." Denver sat back in his chair triumphantly. "They don't have that. For them, time is not stable. Space is not stable. Their own tenuous grasp on this world—that's unstable. It's why they steal the bodies of missing and dead children. The mysterious, impossible, and unsolvable are homing beacons, and so what becomes lost to us becomes found to them. Of course, they're only guessing, too. They just happened to guess right, in this case. They can use our dead to take on physical forms."

Charlie looked away. Tim figured he understood more about what Denver was saying than Mike, whose perplexity etched the expression on his face as he looked from adult to adult.

"Wait, what?" Mike said. "What the hell are you talking about?"

"When people go missing," Charlie said in that grown-up voice, "the rest of us think of them, their whereabouts, as a mystery. We give off a different kind of vibe than those missing people. And all the weird shit that happens in this world, all the shit we think of with the same kind of vibe—those shapes can smell it. They're drawn to it, like the way sharks are drawn to blood. And us," he turned to Mike and the look in his eyes was a smoldering kind of anger, "guys like you and me are almost looked at the same way. Like we're the freaks causing all the freaky stuff in the world."

"Some of you are."

Charlie turned that gaze on Denver, who shrugged and added, "At least, the ones who summoned these things in the first place certainly are."

The look in Charlie's eyes dissipated, and he sighed.

Tim, who had watched the exchange uncomfortably, reached

the limit of his patience. "Great. We've nailed down a why and a how. That's not going to help us end this. If you have a way to help us stop this, Mr. Denver, tell us now. As you pointed out, we're running out of time, here."

"Right, right," Denver replied, rolling back to the computer. "Reversing the spell. Which one of you witnessed the summoning?"

"Uh, I did," Mike said, half-raising his hand.

"C'mere," Denver said. "Explain it all in detail, best as you can remember."

Mike did, starting with the car ride and ending when he went to sleep in his own bed. When he got to the part where Jeremy had taken Charlie's old bones from a bag and Tim's blood from a tissue, Denver groaned a little, but kept silent until Mike was done. Finally, he rolled away from the desk and wheeled around to face the other three.

"We have to get out to that farmhouse," Denver said. "I know the ritual Mike is describing. I suspected it was that one, but Mike's story confirms it. And it's going to be a bitch to reverse, but it can be done. Only one issue, though. Those things were brought forth using blood and bone. We need to use blood and bone to send them back."

There was an uncomfortable pause, and then Tim said, "Well, if you need my blood, you can cut me. Obviously, I'll go along with it. But bone? We can't exactly take more of Charlie's bones."

"Can't we?"

The three turned to Denver, appalled.

"No!" Tim said as if speaking to a willful if somewhat slow child. "Of course not! Absolutely, no way."

"Now wait a minute, wait a minute," Denver said, holding up his hands to placate the others. "Just hear me out, okay? We don't need a lot of bone. Just a fingertip really. We could take the pinkie finger up to the first knuckle. He'd never even miss it?"

"Denver, man, fuck you," Mike said. "We ain't giving you Charlie's finger, dude. Think of something else. Use a chicken bone or something. We could get that a Kroger."

"No can do, Mike-o," Denver said. "Has to be bone from

the same source as the bone used to summon the entities. Otherwise, instead of closing a door, you might well be opening up another one to somewhere else. Somewhere worse."

"No, Denver, it's not going to happen," Tim said emphatically. "We need to find another way."

"We have to use his—"

"We can't, dude, that's like—"

"Has to be Charlie—"

"—not cool, man—"

"I'll do it."

It took a few seconds more of back-and-forth before Charlie's words fully registered. The arguments of the others petered off and they all turned to Charlie.

"I'll do it," Charlie repeated. "Let's just get it over with."

"Are you sure?" Tim asked.

Charlie nodded, stoic. "Let's do it before I change my mind."

SIXTEEN

Mike suggested getting Charlie drunk first to numb the pain, but Tim and—to everyone's surprise, Denver—vetoed the idea. Alcohol would thin Charlie's blood and make his wound bleed more heavily, Tim explained. Denver backed him up. He offered Charlie weed. The boys, who still clung to remnants of the teacher-student/adult-teen dynamic between them and Tim, looked to their former teacher hesitantly.

Tim nodded. "Go ahead, son," he said softly.

Charlie nodded, took the joint Denver offered, and lit up. He held the joint out to Mike, probably by force of habit, and Tim cleared his throat.

Sheepishly, Mike declined, and Charlie drew back his offer.

The three of them watched as the cloud of marijuana smoke swelled and permeated the room. Tim looked for a window and found a small one on the far side of the room. With some effort, he got it open, although it did little to clear the air. Just as Tim thought he might be catching a contact high from all the smoke, Charlie crushed what little was left into a nearby ashtray.

"I...I think...I'm ready," Charlie said, standing and swaying a little. His eyelids drooped sleepily and his voice had sunken into a relaxed monotone.

Denver looked pained, but he took Charlie by the arm and led him upstairs to a small first-floor bathroom. He closed the toilet lid and gestured to Charlie to sit. The boy did so and flopped his left arm on the edge of the sink.

"Stay here with him," Denver said to Mike and Tim. "I'll be right back." He returned a few minutes later with a large butcher knife in one hand and a small iron pot in the other.

Charlie saw the items and simply turned his head.

"I'm sorry," Denver said. "There's no other way."

"I'm ready," Charlie said.

Denver sighed, nodded, and gestured to Charlie's hand, which lay palm down, fingers spread, on the sink at the edge of its basin. "Hold his wrist, if you will," he said to Tim. Then he handed Mike the pot.

"What's this for?" Mike asked.

"Mike," Tim warned, shaking his head.

Charlie glanced at the pot and looked away. "To boil off the skin and stuff, when he...you know. We only need the bone."

Mike paled. "Gotcha."

Denver took a roll of bandages and some hydrogen peroxide from the bathroom medicine cabinet and placed them on the sink. "Ready?"

"Yeah." Charlie curled his other fingers beneath his palm to get them out of the way. His pinkie finger hung over the basin, bracing against its smooth porcelain side. "Don't give me warning. Just do it."

Tim took the boy's wrist. He felt very hot and a little queasy, and chalked it up to guilt. Tim remembered reading somewhere that it was as easy to bite through a finger bone as it was a carrot, and although he'd never, thankfully, had reason to test that, he hoped for Charlie's sake that it was true.

Denver exchanged glances with Tim, and then without warning, he brought the knife down.

Charlie screamed. The blood spurting from the stump where the other half of his pinkie finger used to be was stark crimson against even the aging white of the porcelain. It spattered everywhere. Behind them, Mike groaned and muttered, "Oh God," under his breath.

"Pot," Denver said, and when Mike offered it, he scooped up Charlie's finger just before it rolled down the drain and dropped it into the pot with a little metallic ding.

"Jesus," Mike said, holding the pot away from him. Denver ignored him. He was busy dousing the wound on Charlie's hand with hydrogen peroxide. Charlie screamed louder, his wrist struggling to pull away from Tim's grasp, but Tim held firm.

"Let us fix you first," Tim said, that queasy feeling increasing. "Just hang in there, Charlie. Hang in there."

Denver bandaged up the wound with an expertise born of experience, and Tim found himself wondering what this guy's story was. Once bandaged, Tim let go and Charlie yanked his mutilated hand to his chest, cradling it and whimpering. He didn't cry, Tim noticed, but he did whimper.

"Take two of these," Denver said, handing him two pills. "They're like morphine. All I got right now, but painkillers are being delivered later this evening." At Tim's questioning look, Denver returned a defensive, "I know a guy, okay?"

Tim shrugged in response. "You okay, Charlie? Can we get you something? A glass of water, maybe?"

Charlie bit his lip and shook his head. The color had drained from his face, and he slumped to one side, against the cool tiles of the bathroom wall. "Can I crash on a couch or something for a bit?"

"Take the bed," Denver said. "Come on. I'll help you get there."

The three of them helped Charlie down the hall to a small, sparsely furnished bedroom with a king-sized bed. To Tim's surprise, it was neat, almost military in the way it was made, and the sheets looked clean.

Seeming to understand what Tim was thinking, Denver said, "I just put them on this morning. Clean sheets. Lay down, Charlie. Sleep a bit."

Charlie nodded and, still clutching his hand, tumbled into the bed and closed his eyes. The others filed out of the room, easing the door closed behind them. None of them spoke until they had made their way down to the kitchen and Denver had started a pot of coffee. Mike seemed to remember he was still holding the pot with Charlie's severed finger in it, and hurriedly put it on one of the burners of the stove, wiping his hands on his pants in disgust. Denver took the pot by the handle without a word and nearly filled the pot with water. Then he set it back on the burner and turned the stove on.

Mike clutched his stomach and sank into a kitchen chair next to Tim. "I can't believe we did that."

"We had no choice," Denver said. "It's either those few bones or all of ours, everywhere."

"Which brings me to a question," Tim said, although he was fairly sure he knew the answer. "When are we going to bleed me?"

"Huh?" Mike looked confused.

"Charlie's bones, my blood, right? You've got to cut me, I assume. When?"

"Well, from what Mike tells me, they used dried blood of yours. Leaving aside the fact that it never should have worked in the first place, I think the fact that it did gives us some leeway. Still, fresh blood is better than dried blood. I think we should wait until we're ready. Until we get to the house."

"So we're going back there," Mike said. It was neither a question nor a statement but something in-between.

"Yes, as soon as Charlie feels up to it." Denver poured three mugs of coffee and brought them over to the table.

"So what now?"

"Now," said a voice from somewhere in the kitchen, "you play with us."

SEVENTEEN

What happened to Mike happened very quickly. One minute he was there, looking around for the source of the voice, and the next he was collapsing into himself. To Tim, the boy looked like an origami figure, folded and refolded, or like a shirt being packed into a suitcase. They were insane thoughts, made crazier by an inexplicable desire to laugh at the absurdity of the situation, but horror overtook humor. Mike hovered over the kitchen floor, eyes wide and glazing, hands flopping around uselessly like dying fish. He might have been trying to communicate or maybe he was just spasming by that point. Either way, the grotesqueness of it held Tim and Denver in paralyzed awe. Blood seeped out of Mike's mouth and his bones cracked as his arms and legs folded behind him. His neck bent, and then he was folded in half again, face to groin.

Then he dropped to the ground, and the two dead children behind him glared sullenly at Tim.

"You can't," said the little boy. He looked so much like Tim's little brother that it hurt the heart. It was wrong; it infuriated him...but it hurt more. "You can't send us back."

"You aren't welcome here," Tim said before he realized he was saying it. "You aren't wanted."

"We want *you*," the little girl standing next to the boy said. She, like the other shapes, looked vaguely familiar—a flicker of memory from a milk carton or HAVE YOU SEEN ME? poster. "And Mike." She grinned a great big doll's grin at the twisted lump on the floor that had been Mike. "And Charlie of course."

"What are you?" Denver asked with the calm of a scientist.

His hands shook a little but otherwise, the man was cool as ice. "Why are you here?"

The boy and girl looked at each other, then at Denver. "We want to survive," the girl said.

"We want to live," the boy added.

"We can't go back," said the girl.

"We won't," said the boy. "We will have permanence in this world. We will kill you if you get in our way."

"Some of you, we'll kill anyway."

The girl looked at Denver and he cried out in pain. Half of his forearm, wrist, and hand were bending the wrong way. She took a step toward Tim, her tiny face scrunched in aggressive determination. The boy put a hand on her arm, arresting her approach.

She turned, big eyes flashing, but the boy shook his head. "Not yet," he said. "There's an order. And rules."

The girl considered his words, then nodded.

To Tim, the boy said, "Don't get in our way. The Fractal is coming, and when it does, your silly bones and blood won't make a difference."

Then the two of them disappeared.

For a long time, neither Denver nor Tim spoke. Finally, in a shaky voice, Denver said, "You and the boy are in danger. We're out of time. We need to get Charlie. We have to move." Denver looked around the kitchen as if searching for preparations.

"It said the Fractal was coming."

"What?" Denver asked, pausing in his search.

"It—the boy thing—said the Fractal was coming. What is that?"

Denver shook his head. "Nothing good, I imagine. Those kid-things are only paving the way." He whistled long and low. "Maybe the Fractal is what they're paving the way for."

EIGHTEEN

Mr. Triangle's killing of the boy named Mike had accomplished much. For one, it left them with only one summoner left, the initiator of the ritual, Jeremy, and once he was killed, then only the keys would be left. And so the ritual order of things had been maintained.

The killings had also proved both satisfying and informative. It never ceased to amaze Mr. Triangle how fragile and breakable the creatures of this dimension were. They were easy to kill, for the most part, and their bones made satisfying, almost comforting, crunching sounds when they broke. The killing of the summoners had been invigorating, as Mr. Triangle had promised. They had been able to drink from the wellspring of those souls, and they had learned so much. They had been efficient and swift. They felt more real, more present. Their safety was practically assured.

Miss Circle had said the others had doubts, had been whispering contrarian things. No doubt that was Mr. Hexagon's doing. He wanted the power, the knowledge, the control. He wanted Miss Circle to regard him with affection. Mr. Hexagon had always been a problem. If there was a way to weaken Mr. Triangle's hold on the other shapes, especially Miss Circle, then Mr. Hexagon would exploit it.

Mr. Triangle had told Miss Circle that he wasn't scared, and she had believed him because she hadn't realized she wasn't picking up all his thoughts, only part of them. Partly, Mr. Triangle had done it to see if it could be done. New bodies, new organs of thought, that sort of thing. But he recognized a driving force was in protecting his status—to her as much if not more than to the others. Fear would look weak and uncertain, and the others already worried about whether they would get lost in the chaos the Fractal would bring. Their race had long been scouts for the bigger things subsisting on one dimension after another, and every time, their efforts went largely unacknowledged and their concerns left dangling. The shapes had learned early on that they could trust only each other, and even then, only somewhat, as the idea of bonds between them was a fairly recent development, likely because of exposure to dimensions where such things mattered. They were practical, survival-oriented. They took pleasure in small things, the newness of the little details of different worlds, and that was often a solitary, contemplative state of being. But here, in this world, with bonds between creatures so important a thing, it had affected them. They had begun maneuverings to solidify such bonds and also to overthrow and replace them, and Mr. Triangle found the latter threatening.

He was scared. He had reason to be.

With the Fractal coming, things would happen fast, and if it devolved the world before the shapes could complete the killing of the keys, they might very well still be sent back. The Fractal wouldn't be affected, but they certainly would, and in the flux their prior dimension was in, they would likely be torn apart.

Mr. Triangle's mind kept returning to the idea of bonds, to the notion of loyalty. Would the others stand behind him, even if it meant going against, detaining, or delaying the Fractal? Would Miss Circle? And why did her loyalty matter to him so much more than the others'?

He thought, too, about the body he had resurrected. Apparently, it had been connected somehow to the key called Tim. Mr. Triangle could feel recognition and a deep, dull pain coming from Tim when he looked at the body Mr. Triangle was using, and that was interesting. He had felt the concept of "brother," a biological and familial connection, and an accompanying affection. It was not the same kind of connection Mr. Triangle felt for Miss Circle, but it was powerful. It would be useful.

Mr. Hexagon's thought broke into his own, interrupting

him, but Mr. Triangle found he could mask his annoyance at such things much better in these bodies.

It's taking its time certainly, Mr. Hexagon thought at him. *The Fractal—it is usually much less restrained in breaking through. Is this world so much harder to cross into for it?*

The question was not presented as an earnest inquiry for knowledge so much as a musing only half-offered to Mr. Triangle. He chose to address it anyway.

Every time it crosses into a new dimension, its sanity devolves a little. This would be our fifth world. I think the Fractal is falling apart, at least in terms of its cognitive faculties.

It's unstable, then.

Yes. Mr. Triangle saw no point in lying, not when Mr. Hexagon was probing his thoughts like that.

That is bad for us.

No. Mr. Triangle glanced at Mr. Hexagon. *It is good. It means the Fractal is confused, disorganized. It is directionless chaotic energy. It buys us time to finish our work here.*

Unless it comes through now.

Mr. Triangle didn't answer right away. He ought to have; his mental silence put forth the idea that the concerns Mr. Hexagon was raising were valid. Finally, he thought, *The rift isn't wide enough. It needs to bang its head a few more times against the door before it can break through, and sometimes, it forgets it is even doing that.*

Mr. Hexagon shrugged. It was a gesture he had picked up which infuriated Mr. Triangle. It was, for one, a gesture he hadn't mastered—he looked like those broken bodies when he tried it—and it denoted everything from disbelief to disinterest, and Mr. Hexagon used it for both. When Mr. Triangle turned on his little boy's heels, though, the cold dark in his eyes still had its intended potency. Despite his child-body being nearly a head taller than Mr. Triangle's, Mr. Hexagon took a step back.

Tell the others we are ready. We kill the last summoner now. All of us. And we make it a glorious example.

Mr. Hexagon turned without another thought and went to

gather the others. Mr. Triangle watched the colors of the rift, and for a single moment, felt an intense, sharp, almost painful spike of hate. Whether it was for Mr. Hexagon or for the Fractal, he wasn't quite sure, but it felt good. It felt like strength. It felt like the time before, when bonds did not matter and survival was the reigning principle of their existences.

Perhaps not all shapes would see the conquering of the new world. Mr. Triangle reached out and stroked the edges of the rift. He couldn't actually physically feel them with the dead-child's fingers, but he enjoyed connecting to the substance of the rift anyway.

It worked both ways, the rift. Shapes who had outlived their usefulness could be tossed back through, made examples of. And there were ways to close it, too, before or after the emergence of the Fractal.

Maybe, just maybe, the shapes, with Mr. Triangle in a position of authority, could rule a dimension of their own.

NINETEEN

While Denver was downstairs gathering supplies, Tim tried to wake Charlie. The boy was bleeding a little through the bandage and mumbling in his sleep, but when Tim shook his shoulder, his eyelids only fluttered, and he began to snore lightly.

"Charlie," Tim said. "Get up. Come on, we have to get out of here." Tim's voice, he realized, was softer than was useful for waking the boy up, but Tim couldn't shake the feeling that they were being watched, or at least listened to. Maybe it was an aftershock of what had been done to Mike, a delayed horror at the brutality of his death. Tim wasn't sure. But it seemed important just then to get Charlie out of there with as little fuss and noise as possible.

He reached out toward Charlie's shoulder again when there was a blinding flash of light inside his head, and a sharp crack he felt across his skull as much as heard in his ears. The familiar hot flash and vague dizziness followed; he was having a vision.

In it, he saw snapshots of images, strung together in a kind of mental garland of ideas.

He saw a bright yellow glow, and within it, an endless swirl of grinding teeth.

He saw Charlie without an arm and Denver sliced in half from skull to groin.

He saw the bodies of dead children twisting out of shape.

He saw Jeremy's teeth yanked out of his head and his fingers broken by sizzling tendrils of electricity.

He saw a world torn apart by a moving black hole.

Then the flash of light and heat snapped off and the dizziness was replaced by a bone-deep buzzing, a kind of vibration that made him nauseous.

"Jenks?"

Tim blinked hard to bring the world back into focus. Charlie was looking up at him sleepily. He looked pale.

"We've got to go," Tim said. They were the only words he could manage to send from brain to mouth.

"What happened?"

Tim shook his head. "Charlie, get up. I'll explain in the car." He didn't have it in him to tell Charlie yet about Mike, but Charlie seemed to sense the gravity of the situation anyway. Without further questions, he got up and slipped on his sneakers. Tim led him back downstairs, where Denver was waiting with a few duffel bags in the hallway.

"Where's Mike?" Charlie asked. He was still sleepy enough that he didn't sound alarmed, even as he took in the uncomfortable glance Tim and Denver exchanged.

"Come on," Denver said, hoisting up two of the three duffel bags. Tim took the third.

"Jenks? Mr. Jenkins, where's Mike?"

They went out into the dusk.

"He's gone, Charlie," Tim finally said. "The shapes came, and…." He couldn't finish. Glancing back, he saw that Charlie was taking in what Tim had told him.

"They killed him?" Charlie finally asked.

"Afraid so," Denver replied. He, too, seemed uneasy with meeting the boy's gaze.

"Jesus," Charlie muttered. "So now what?"

"They're going after Jeremy," Denver said. "If they kill that boy, then you and Tim are next. Then…who knows. That rip you told me about opens wide, and…who knows."

"So, we have to rescue that asshole, then?"

As they piled into the car, Tim stifled a laugh. It would have sounded crazy even to him—it would have been crazy—but he understood the irony Charlie was getting at.

"If possible," Denver said before Tim could answer. "And then, we have to find a way to sew up that rip."

Denver drove, following as best he could the half-offered

directions to Jeremy's house from Charlie in the back seat. When they arrived at the house, the warm glow of sunset had cooled to a blue-black.

Denver took another, much smaller bag from the glove compartment.

"What's that?" Tim asked.

The grizzled man looked down at it—a dark velvet pouch with a drawstring—and said, "Think of it like a gun. Or a condom. Better to have it and not need it than to need it and not have it." Before getting out of the car, he tossed the velvet pouch to Tim, who caught it as if it was breakable or easily ignitable. It might have been either, as far as Tim knew.

He and Charlie got out of the car and hurried to catch up to Denver, who was stalking across the lawn toward the backyard gate with one of the duffel bags in hand.

"We're going around back?"

Denver nodded, and gestured toward the glow and crackle coming from beyond the fence. "The would-be devil worshipper has a fire going over there."

They pushed through the gate and into a yard in a sad state of neglect. What might have once been a garden under one of the back windows was overgrown with weeds and crabgrass. A shredded tire lay in one back corner of the yard by a dilapidated shed. Near a small patio leading up to a rickety-looking back deck, a small fire pit choked with branches and small logs held just about the only robust thing in the yard—a blazing fire. Two folding chairs had been set up by the fire amidst the rubble of old beer cans, but no one was sitting in them. In fact, so far as Tim could see, no one was in the yard at all. The house looked dark.

"Shit," Denver muttered. "I was sure he'd—"

"What the fuck are you doing here?" a voice said from behind them, and all three of them jumped, turning around.

Jeremy stood there, holding a beer. He looked terrible. His eyes were glossy with a crazed mix of anger and fear. His hair was a tangle in his face, he had a bruise on his cheek and a busted lip. The gash in the side of his face was crusted over with a bloody scab. The front of his shirt was torn. It took a moment for Tim to realize the beer can Jeremy was holding was crushed, and a jagged piece of aluminum can must have sunken into the flesh of Jeremy's palm, because it wasn't condensation or even beer dripping from his grip.

"We're here to save you, asshole," Charlie muttered, still dazed, and giggled to himself.

"You dumbasses," Jeremy said, walking toward the fire. "Now you just gave them all the people they want to kill in one place. We're fucked."

"You're welcome," Charlie said.

"The fuck is with him?"

Charlie held up his injured hand. "Been running around trying to undo the shit you did."

Jeremy's crazed look faded some. "They're going to kill us all."

"No," Denver said. "They're not. We just have to send them back."

The anger flared in Jeremy's eyes again, and Tim briefly wondered what sustained the heat of that energy. A lot of the kids he taught let things about their pasts, their family, or their experiences slip once in a while. Tim heard things, and it made him more sympathetic toward them. He didn't know anything about Jeremy, other than that his brother seemed a little slow. The other kids didn't seem to know much, either. Whatever Jeremy's baggage was, whatever made that anger flow so freely and so intensely, it was something he kept tightly to himself.

"And what the fuck would you know about it?"

Unphased, Denver said, "You'd be surprised," and he set down the duffel bag. "This ain't my first time dealing with this sort of shit, kid. But you can bet your fucking ass I plan to make it the last, if I can."

He unzipped the duffel bag.

TWENTY

Denver reached into the bag and started laying an assortment of guns on the ground beside it. Then he started pulling out old leatherbound books, large medallions with ghastly faces, and different faintly luminescent powders in Ziploc bags.

"What...what is all that?" Charlie asked, absently cradling his bandaged hand with his good one. Tim could tell from the way he was shivering slightly that the pain meds were wearing off.

Denver didn't answer until he had produced a knife and then Charlie's boiled finger bones in a small plasticware box. He looked up at Charlie and said, "Tools of the trade, boy. Now, we're going to need some of your friend's blood there." He gestured at Tim.

"Are those bones?" Jeremy smiled. The gesture was so lacking in anything like human empathy or emotion that it made Tim distinctly uneasy. This boy was truly dangerous—not because he went looking to cause pain and destruction, but because he simply didn't feel enough for anyone to care whether pain and destruction was caused. That he had unleashed those little monsters on the world surprised Tim only in that he'd managed to focus on and show interest in any one thing long enough that it had actually worked. And despite the fact that he was as much a boy physically as Charlie was or Mike had been, Tim realized with dismay that he was already lost. It happened sometimes— much less often than many of his colleagues might believe— that nature and genetics and circumstance created sociopathic and even psychopathic men in children's bodies, people who were born without that crucial piece in their minds that linked certain actions with guilt or sadness or fear. It wasn't that they didn't recognize actions had consequences; it was that nothing about those consequences perturbed them in the slightest.

In a way Jeremy scared Tim more than the shapes did.

"Yeah," Charlie said to Jeremy, waving his bandaged hand.

"Like the ones you stole," Tim added. "For your ritual."

Jeremy's eyes took on a faraway look that was impossible to read. "I didn't know it would work." It wasn't a defense so much as an observation. "It never should have."

"Well, it did. You really screwed the pooch on this one," Denver said, rising with the knife.

"They killed my brother," Jeremy said without emotion, that faraway look sharpening, coming into focus. Tim still couldn't read it, but he didn't like it. "Those shapes. The ones who look like children."

"I'm sorry to hear that," Denver said.

"Don't be. He was a brain-damaged retard anyway." Jeremy smiled again. "They did him a favor. Maybe they'll do the same for you."

"Why are we saving this asshole again?" Charlie muttered.

Jeremy turned on him. "They want you. You and Jenks. And me. So they can stay here. I can hear their thoughts sometimes. Then we're all dead and maybe that's fucking better."

"You're a crazy motherfucker, you know that?" Charlie glared at him, and for a moment, Tim thought the boy might hit the leering little sociopath. Jeremy towered over Charlie and had a violent temper, but Charlie probably had ten pounds of muscle on Jeremy and a temper of his own.

"If you've got a problem, douchebag, come at me," Jeremy said, thumping his chest. "I don't mind beating you down so it's easier for them to take you. You think those finger bones are all they want? They'll strip your skin off and crush up the rest of you and drink you like soup." Then Jeremy threw his head back and let out a wild bark of laughter. "You're a dead man, Charlie," he said in between panting breaths. "We all are."

The wind shifted then, growing colder, and Jeremy stopped laughing. He looked excited, though, as he looked around the yard.

Tim and the others became aware, by degrees, that they were surrounded. The pale children, with their serious little faces from missing posters and their anachronistic clothes, had formed a circle around them. He estimated about nine of them and found that he inexplicably knew their names. Mr. Triangle, who looked so much like his brother, and Miss Circle, the girl from the club.

Mr. Square stood next to her, and Mr. Rhombus next to him, then Ms. Oval, Mr. Rectangle, Ms. Trapezoid, Miss Octagon, and back round to Mr. Hexagon, the boy from the newspaper article. But his gaze focused on the one using his brother's dead body, plucked from another time and space.

"Jeremy, it's time," Mr. Triangle said. He looked as if he was sensing something in the night air. "Time is growing short."

"The Fractal is coming soon, isn't it?" Jeremy said.

"Soon," Mr. Hexagon replied.

"And you, the one called Mr. Denver," Miss Circle added, "can watch."

"No, I don't think so," Denver said, grabbing Tim's wrist. "It's time for you to go back." And then he cut Tim's palm wide open with the knife.

TWENTY-ONE

The shapes closed ranks. Mr. Triangle stepped closer to them, with Mr. Hexagon right behind him. They looked so small to Tim in their child-bodies, and when Mr. Triangle made a tiny, pale fist, Tim almost laughed.

Then Jeremy screamed. It sounded strange, maybe because it was so thin, so full of terror, and therefore so very much unlike any sound Tim could imagine Jeremy making. The sound seemed to go on long after it should have, one long, loud, continuous wail. Mr. Triangle's little fist had turned bone white, paler even than the dead hue of his skin. He shook it a little, and tight red seams formed up and down Jeremy's arms and down the center of his face. A faint grinding sound came from somewhere beneath the boy's face, and a second later, Jeremy's head caved in. His arms followed suit as the bones inside splintered, poking up through the surface of his skin in tiny slivers before the arms shriveled and rolled up to the elbows. Then the rest of him began to collapse in on itself, a bloody origami project of grotesque folding and refolding.

Tim had a horrible mental flash of the club in which he'd first found Charlie, with the litter of bodies mangled and twisted into horrible distortions. As he watched, part of Jeremy's spine either shifted or disintegrated, and the torso curved backward until his crumpled head emerged from between his denim legs. Blood splattered and hissed on the faintly burning fire. It pooled beneath the body, which was becoming more unrecognizable by the minute. A wad of loosed flesh, soaked red, landed on the toe of Tim's shoe.

The boy's jeans split along the lengths of the thighs down to the buckling knees. The femurs burst from their encasements of flesh and the thing that used to be Jeremy collapsed in a heap on the grass.

Tim, who had been appalled by the scene before him, hadn't been able to take in anything else going on around him. Now, he noticed the sound of Denver feverishly muttering behind him and turned to see the man tossing powders into the flames as he read from one of the musty books.

Charlie stood close by. He, too, had been mesmerized by the atrocity of Jeremy's death, and now that the bloody, mangled heap lay motionless on the grass, he turned toward Tim and Denver.

"Guys? If you have a plan beyond mumbling over old books, now might be the time to get it going."

Neither man answered. Denver's voice had taken on a kind of chanting quality, and although it never rose in volume or pitch, it had certainly increased in intensity. Tim glanced uneasily at the shapes. They were watching Denver with a peculiar mix of fascination and fear.

Mr. Hexagon turned to Mr. Triangle. "Why aren't you killing him?" he asked, and Tim thought he detected a note of disdain in the boyish voice—a voice which was strange in its coldness.

Mr. Triangle turned to the speaker. The hate behind his eyes was barely contained. Tim, who had spent years observing the subtle art of communication among his students, thought he detected a weak spot in their ranks.

"Try it," Mr. Triangle said. "Try to kill him while he's reciting a blocking spell. See what happens."

"He'll ruin our plans," Mr. Hexagon said.

"Don't let him send us back," Miss Circle said from behind them. Her voice sounded pleading.

"It's too late for him to stop us," Mr. Triangle said placidly. "We are not alone now."

To Tim's left, Charlie muttered, "Oh fuck." Tim looked in the direction of Charlie's gaze.

What he saw made him stagger back. Behind the children, a mass, within which was a self-contained thunderstorm, was taking shape. All around them, the children-things hummed with excitement.

The Fractal had come.

TWENTY-TWO

Denver mumbled furiously as the storm cloud behind the shapes took form. Flashes of lightning within the nebulae splintered off again and again and again in infinite bright-to-fading light. The amorphous colors formed shapes that peeled and whirled off into smaller versions of themselves, over and over. The effect was dizzying and surprisingly nauseating. Tim suspected it was the clash of colors within, the unceasing movement...and the undercurrent of hatred which seemed to curdle the very air around it.

"It's come," Mr. Hexagon said, his dead-child's eyes focused on the mass. Tim couldn't tell from the boy-thing's tone or expression if the feeling among the shapes was one of awe or fear. He suspected it was a little of both.

"It won't let the humans send us back, right?" Miss Circle, who had joined Mr. Hexagon and Mr. Triangle, tugged on the latter's sleeve.

"No," Mr. Triangle agreed. "Of course it won't." To Tim, he said, "Now, the Fractal will do what we can't."

"Denver?" Charlie uttered in a low voice. He had that strange feral look on his face again, the one Tim didn't like. Didn't trust. "I can feel it in my head. It knows me. It's always known me. Us."

"What's it saying?" Tim asked, but he thought he knew. He thought a strange narration, rising and falling in tone and volume, an endless ebb and flow of words, had begun to accompany the visions spiking through his head. There were endless blooming wounds, patterns of rot repeating in ever-smaller scale. There were inward spirals of toxic galaxies where dead children were the least of all horrors. And there were the words, talking about the ones who had gone missing, the ones who had been abducted, the ones who lay in cold, dark earth or at the bottom of darker, colder bodies of water. There were little bodies never discovered, bodies that had fallen to dust and bone, and the shapes had found and restored them. The shapes had taken and reshaped like them clay, had filled them with essence and life and power humans could never know. Words tumbled in over those sentiments, washing over them, spilling over them, rushing past them like sound past a cave opening, and the new words talked of worlds lost and forgotten, worlds left to fall to dust and ash that the Fractal had resurrected. The Fractal, who could create or destroy with the words of the Oldest Ones, the Fractal who devoured worlds and remade them in its image.

Tim didn't think the Fractal was consciously relaying its nature or its plans to him and Charlie. Rather, it seemed like it was simply exploring their minds and in turn, opening its own up as a matter of course. What it was, what it intended to do, what it *could* do, was so far beyond anything that even the shapes could imagine. They were violent, capricious, willful, anxious little things, but they were, in a sense, really just children, terrified of losing substance and significance.

The Fractal, on the other hand, was scared of nothing.

Denver's mumbling had taken on a feverish intensity. Though Tim couldn't make out the words, the sentiment was clear. He was trying to banish the thing, and with it, its cult of small monsters, but he was running out of time.

Still, Tim thought he noticed a faint glow around Denver's shoulders. It could have been a corona of distortion from the pain behind Tim's eyes, but he didn't think so. He hoped whatever Denver was doing was finally starting to work.

As the Fractal expanded, its patterns swirling outward before collapsing in on itself to start again, the shapes backed away, forming a line just beneath it. Tim could still hear the pour of words in his head, the soundless formations of thought, and an idea occurred to him.

The shapes couldn't hear what the Fractal was telling him

and Charlie. If they could, they would have moved—they would have run. They huddled beneath it, though, like young animals to a mother, as it told Tim it didn't need them anymore, that their usefulness was done.

Their grim, solemn looks, so serious on children's faces, turned one by one into masks of surprise and horror. From the edges of the line inward, the dead avatars of the shapes began to fall apart.

Tim's stomach lurched as the skin of their faces became dry and papery and peeled away, glimmering for a minute like ash before winking out. What were the plump, fleshy faces of children grew rough, then skeletal, and the contagion spread down their little bodies. Without the confines of human structure to contain them, the sludgy silver forms beneath stretched and snapped, distorting, pinching, then stretching again amid screams which became wails which became the unearthly siren sounds of a betrayed and dying race. Within minutes, only three of them stood—Miss Circle, looking terrified, Mr. Hexagon, looking angry, and Mr. Triangle, who wore no expression at all. Miss Circle went next, the same as the others only much slower, and Tim thought he could see genuine pain in the boy-faces of the remaining two shapes, especially Mr. Triangle. Mr. Hexagon followed, and then Tim understood that what he saw was derision and disappointment, as if with his last dying breath, the shape refused to wail in fear but chose instead to judge in silence.

When Mr. Hexagon was gone, Mr. Triangle turned to Tim and Charlie. "Kill it," he said. And then, within minutes, the rage of the Fractal had disintegrated him, too. Tim wretched, sucking in deep breaths to keep from vomiting. It was his brother falling apart—no, that wasn't true. His brother had died long ago. But it was his brother's face that was wasting away and shriveling. The pain on it had become something complex and adult, and Tim couldn't help but wonder if all children exposed to such horror and betrayal as murder looked, in those final moments, the same way.

"Denver!" Charlie cried out. Without the distractions of the shapes, the Fractal was free to turn its full attention on the remaining humans. A pale light the color of the rip had enveloped Charlie and was lifting him off the ground. "Denver, for fuck's sake!"

"Seriously, man," Tim said, staggering toward Denver. He dropped to one knee. The pain in his head bloomed into something enormous, consuming everything in its harsh brightness.

He reached out a hand toward Denver's shoulder, and when he made contact with the man, he suddenly saw the universe.

TWENTY-THREE

The world before Tim—the back yard, Charlie, Denver, all of it—was gone. Tim was floating in space, surrounded by a reddish light. Before him sprawled endless swirling galaxies and countless planets torn apart and pulled back together again, hurtling around blazing suns on the verge of supernova.

And then, just as suddenly, he was back again on his knees in the damp grass, in the summer dark of Jeremy Clinton's back yard. Denver's forehead glittered with beads of sweat. His eyes were closed so tightly they looked as if they could cause his face to fold in on itself. His lips moved with silent, feverish intensity. Above him and to his left, Charlie still hung suspended in mid-air, kicking and cursing and trying to wriggle out of whatever invisible grasp held him.

"Denver!" Charlie cried out, and then he was flung across the yard.

"Oh my God!" Tim breathed, and stumbled in his attempts to stand up and go after the boy. Before he could get far, a hand grabbed him, its strength biting into his forearm.

Tim looked down to see Denver, and this time his face didn't just suggest collapse, but was collapsing. The skin had pulled so tight that it had begun to tear around his jawline, and as it broke free, it snapped wetly toward his eyes. Every place the skin was exposed, it was stretching and snapping, stretching and snapping, like some terrible tide. Denver gestured to the Fractal.

The cloud still flashed lightning while its colors danced off in repeating patterns. He could still feel its hate...but it was weakening. It was lashing out at Denver, who had been using powerful words against it, words it didn't think the creatures of this dimension even knew about, let alone knew how to use. Those words, Tim felt the storm cloud thinking, might well be stronger than the blood and bone.

The grasp on Tim's forearm loosened, and he turned in time to see a red, glistening, skinless thing slump to the ground. Tim couldn't look at it. He couldn't focus on it. All he could get his brain to register was the tiny smear of blood on the open page of the book Denver had been reading from.

The book.

Tim snatched it, then glared up at the Fractal.

It pulsed hate.

He looked down at the pages, and for a terrible moment, utter despair set in. He wasn't even sure the lines and squiggles were meant to be words. They hurt his eyes, seeming to lean out from the page. What did he think he was doing? He was no magician. He was a dead man with useless paper in his hands. He couldn't decipher the language of the book, let alone read the spells within. He thought of Charlie, and then of his wife. He'd failed them both.

Suddenly, the glyphs resolved themselves into words he could read, or at least interpret and translate.

He frowned, confused. How had—

Then he understood. It was the Fractal. It had connected with him, had opened channels of understanding that it still didn't seem to realize went both ways. Tim could understand the words simply because the Fractal could. It didn't seem to understand just yet, but it was giving him the ability to send it away.

Tim began to read.

TWENTY-FOUR

Fervently, he began to speak the words out loud, soft at first but growing louder. Around him, a whirlwind of air had sprung up, lashing at his clothes, his face, his ears, stuffing them with muted sound so that Tim had to shout to hear himself. He glanced up once and saw the Fractal stretching and compressing, splitting open in some places and melting together in others. Where the rips in the creature had formed, the rushing wind poured out, and it had begun to sound like screams. There was light, too, inside the creature, a cold, burning brightness that Tim knew to be raw pain, the manifestation of the words spilling out of him. Those words were tearing the thing apart.

Tim read faster, louder, the words forming their own rushing, screaming sound, and Tim could suddenly feel the pain of them. The Fractal was sharing that, too. What it felt, Tim felt. Its death throes, its cessation of existence—Tim could feel it all.

In the periphery of his vision, as his gaze flew over the words on the pages, he could see his own hands splitting open, filling with cold light and rushing air. The skin around those openings faded.

His thoughts flickered to his wife again, but then he tried to dispel them quickly. It was too late, though. The Fractal had seen, and returned images of engulfing her in rage that ripped the skin from her bones and then twisted those bones into the most awful shapes....

Faster, louder—Tim's throat ached from screaming the words in their strange language, a tongue which itself threatened to twist the throat. He didn't think he could stop now if he wanted to. His body was working independently of his thoughts and feelings. The words were their own thing now, using him to be born into the world and to take the Fractal out of it.

He felt its hate...and its sudden realization that the words it had always known were not words the Tim-creature knew by nature or study. It only knew them because—

Tim read faster, faster.

Suddenly, the light behind his eyes went out, and all sound ceased entirely. The words left him, and without them to hold him up, he sank to the ground. It knew, it *knew!* The Fractal had cut off its connection to Tim, and now, weakened because the Fractal was, he had nothing left in him to fight back with. His eyes—were they open or closed?—couldn't see. He couldn't hear. He couldn't even really feel the ground beneath him except as coldness...against his cheek, his neck, through his clothes. And then that faded, too, and he felt nothing at all.

He might have passed out then, for minutes although it probably wasn't even that long. When his consciousness returned to him, the first thing he felt was grass against his face. It gave him a sense of orientation; he was lying down. He sucked in a breath, and both his throat and chest felt torn up. The pain was a cold, dry thing inside him. The next thing he was aware of was that depthless darkness behind his eyelids, and he opened his eyes.

He rolled over, groaning. Once he managed to sit up, he looked around.

Denver's body was gone, as was Jeremy's. However, the Fractal was gone, too. The dead children, the shapes from another dimension, were gone as well. And Charlie—

"Charlie!" He got unsteadily to his feet, his head aching as it snapped around, looking for signs of the boy. "Charlie! Where are you?"

He spotted his former student lying on the ground several feet away, curled up with his back to the carnage. Tim tried to run over to him. His legs were numb and refused to stand solidly under him, so he crawled to Charlie, his voice reduced to a croak as he called out the boy's name.

Tim had convinced himself Charlie was dead until, about a foot away, he heard a soft groan.

"Charlie!" The voice that came from his throat in a faint mist of blood didn't sound like his own, but he used it anyway. "Charlie, you okay?"

The boy rolled over. His face was heavily bruised on one side, and his injured hand was bleeding through the bandages. He rubbed what might well have been a broken rib with his good hand and coughed.

"Shit," he whispered, and sat up with effort. "Jenks? Where—where is it?"

"Gone. They're all gone."

"Denver?"

Tim didn't answer, but the look on his face must have conveyed the answer. Charlie looked sadly back toward the place where they'd all faced down the lesser gods of a dimension so terrible even those gods were afraid to return to it. His eyes shined for a moment with the beginnings of tears, but he mashed them away with his good hand.

"It's all...they're all gone," he repeated.

"Yeah."

"Can we go? Can we get out of here? I want to go." Charlie spoke softly, and Tim was reminded again that Charlie was still just a kid.

Tim helped him up, and they hobbled back to Tim's car. All around them, the houses were silent. There was an unreal quality to it, as if somehow Tim and Charlie weren't completely there, not totally a part of their surroundings. Maybe that was true, in a way. Certainly, both of them had been touched by something outside of their known universe. They'd been connected to it, a part of it for however brief a time.

Maybe something had been lost in that exchange...or gained. Maybe it was the price of the spell working that a portion of what made them a part of this world would have to be sacrificed. He thought of his wife and wondered....

"I'm sure she's fine," Charlie said, and then, realizing nothing in context to his statement had been spoken aloud, he gave Tim a surprised look.

"Let's go see," Tim said. "You can crash on our couch, get some sleep."

Charlie looked grateful. "Thanks, man. I—I don't think I'm ready to go home. I...I don't know if it's still there. I mean, it's still physically there, probably, but I don't know if it's home." He looked dismayed at being unable to articulate his feelings better.

"It's okay. We'll see. We'll find out."

They got in the car and Tim began to drive toward the oncoming dawn.

It was rising in the west.

ABOUT THE AUTHOR

Mary SanGiovanni is American horror and thriller writer of over a dozen books, including The Hollower trilogy, Chills, and Behind the Door, as well as numerous short stories and non-fiction. She has been nominated for a Bram Stoker Award (The Hollower, which has been cited as an inspiration for Slenderman), and the winner of the Lavinia Kohl Award for Excellence in Literature and the NeCon Legend Award. She has the distinction of being one of the first women to speak about writing at the CIA Headquarters in Langley, VA. She has a Masters degree in Writing Popular Fiction from Seton Hill University, Pittsburgh, where she studied under genre greats. She is currently a member of The Authors Guild, The International Thriller Writers, and Penn Writers.
Bibliography

Curious about other Crossroad Press books?
Stop by our site:
http://store.crossroadpress.com
We offer quality writing
in digital, audio, and print formats.

www.ingramcontent.com/pod-product-compliance
Lightning Source LLC
Chambersburg PA
CBHW022031170626
46808CB00003B/1138